CRISPR'd

CRISPR'd

Nonfiction by Judy Foreman:

Exercise is Medicine, 2020
The Global Pain Crisis, 2017
A Nation in Pain, 2014

CRISPR'd

A MEDICAL THRILLER

JUDY FOREMAN

Skyhorse Publishing

Skyhorse Publishing books may be purchased in bulk at special discounts
for sales promotion, corporate gifts, fund-raising, or educational purposes.
Special editions can also be created to specifications. For details, contact
the Special Sales Department, Arcade Publishing, 307 West 36th Street,
11th Floor, New York, NY 10018 or info@skyhorsepublishing.com.

Skyhorse® and Skyhorse Publishing® are registered trademarks of Skyhorse
Publishing, Inc.®, a Delaware corporation.

Visit our website at www.skyhorsepublishing.com.

10 9 8 7 6 5 4 3 2 1

Library of Congress Cataloging-in-Publication Data is available on file.

Print ISBN: 978-1-5107-6993-9
Ebook ISBN: 978-1-5107-7035-5

Printed in the United States of America

TO SALLY

PROLOGUE

LATE SUMMER 2018

The mourners gathered under the tent in the Mount Auburn Cemetery in Cambridge, forming a protective circle around the freshly dug hole in the ground.

The two sets of grandparents, in their late sixties, stood opposite each other on either side of the grave, the women's dress heels sinking into the wet earth. One of the men held his wife's elbow, trying, despite everything, to be in control, his jaw tightening but his lips quivering. He tried not to look down where their first grandchild lay in a pint-sized casket in front of them.

As for the parents, you could tell that they had once been a handsome couple, she with the face of the model she once was, he with the beginning of distinguished white hair. But today, in the gray mist, their faces were so aged with grief that they looked as old as their own parents. A few friends, cousins, aunts, and uncles completed the circle, tissues soggy with a mixture of raindrops and tears, raincoats soaked through on their shoulders.

After the prayers, the mother, summoning more courage than she thought she had, took the shovel and dug into the wet ground, throwing the earth onto the tiny coffin that had been placed gently at the bottom of the grave. Her hands shook, barely able to hang on to the shovel. She paused for a moment, eyes squeezed shut, hardly breathing. The casket, barely two feet long and one foot wide, looked absurdly small in this enormous cemetery filled with the bodies of people who had lived almost a century longer than the toddler in the coffin.

Stepping back from the edge of the grave, the mother collapsed in her husband's arms, almost sinking to her knees in the muck. Her parents moved closer, helping to keep her upright.

Then it was her husband's turn to shovel dirt onto his son's tiny coffin.

"Why us?" the mourners heard him whisper. "Why us?"

1

JANUARY 2020

"Please raise your right hand. Do you solemnly swear or affirm that you will listen to this case and render a true verdict and a fair sentence as to this defendant?"

As the judge swore in the jury, Samantha Fuller sat, laptop at the ready, in the front row, flanked by dozens of reporters from the Associated Press, *New York Times*, *Washington Post*, *Los Angeles Times*, CNN, the major networks, and a lone reporter each from the BBC and Al Jazeera. In the moments before the judge entered, Sammie had been bombarded by compliments and detailed questions from the other journalists. Sammie hoped she was gracious enough, knowing she would always keep her best stuff to herself.

Jury selection had dragged on for days. The usual disorganized group of average citizens arrived with books, laptops, cell phones, and lunches and sat on hard benches in the Dedham, Massachusetts, courthouse, waiting for their turn to be called.

A few, mostly those in jobs they hated, were eager to be selected for the "CRISPR" trial, as the international press had dubbed the case. Most others, including young parents and people with upcoming vacation plans, silently hoped to be dismissed as soon as possible.

Some were even calling it the "trial of the century," no understatement given the screaming mobs outside.

Eileen O'Connor, the hotshot young defense attorney, was taking her time, hoping to pack the jury with as many nonparents as she could, ideally those who seemed to like the defendant and had favorable views of the world-class fertility clinic where, for years, infertile couples had flocked in desperation.

On the other side of the courtroom, District Attorney Paula Vasquez was also taking her sweet time, trying to do just the opposite: seat as many young parents, preferably women, as she could, to maximize antipathy to the defendant.

Not surprisingly, it had proven nearly impossible to find potential jurors who had not heard of the case. Sammie liked to think that was thanks to her numerous front-page stories covering the case in the *Boston Times*.

Eventually, a jury of eight women and four men, plus two alternates, a man and a woman, were seated and instructed, in formal language, to kiss their normal lives goodbye for the immediate future. They were sequestered in the nearby Hilton, courtesy of the state of Massachusetts, and strictly ordered not to check the news on their TV or any of their devices.

So here they were on a bright Monday morning. The jury and alternates took their seats promptly at 9 a.m. As expected, the courtroom was packed.

In the row behind Sammie sat her friends, her husband Bob, and her kids, Liam and Beau, who, she figured, would learn more in the next few days or weeks in a courtroom than they would in school. In the row behind them sat the tightly bonded group of women who had gone through in vitro fertilization, more commonly referred to as IVF, together at the fertility clinic. The rest of the courtroom was full of legal scholars, historians, and regular folk, all of whom had lined up for hours just to get in.

In the hallway, just outside the courtroom doors, sat an older woman shrouded in a black shawl and, had Sammie stopped to notice, sorrow etched in deep lines around her eyes and mouth. If she had thought about it, Sammie could easily have guessed who the woman was. If anyone had asked the woman if she were related to the defendant, she would probably have said, "No, no, no. No relation. Just interested."

Inside the courtroom, a disheveled man, who had obviously been told to remove his baseball cap, which he was now squeezing viciously in his right hand, sat in the very last row. His jeans were stained, his shirt crumpled. Had Sammie turned around, she would have seen that it was Joe Green, the former night city editor at her old paper, the *Lowell Daily*, the guy who had tried to kill her.

PAULA VASQUEZ NEARLY leapt out of her seat when the judge called for opening statements.

Overconfidence had wrecked many a prosecutor's case, she warned herself. Glancing to her assistants at the prosecution table, she mouthed, "Here we go."

She strode over to the jury, making eye contact with each member, in turn. She stood erect. Her high heels, already killing her feet, gave her an extra three inches of authority, not that she needed it. Her Armani suit clung tightly, but not too tightly, the skirt skimming her knees. It was black, not funereal, but somber. The white blouse underneath allowed just a hint of cleavage. She was professional, her outfit proclaimed, but female, too, like the grieving mothers she would soon put on the stand.

She gestured to the easels with the pictures of the deceased children and to the children's grandparents sitting behind the lawyers at the prosecution table. The parents were scheduled to testify and were not in the courtroom yet. The grandparents' faces were eloquent, silently begging the jurors to put the defendant away forever.

"The state will show that the defendant committed premeditated murder, that the defendant's actions directly resulted in the deaths of three infants, Jamie Northrup, Katy Graf Wilson, and Henry Steinberg. Our evidence will also show that nine other infants were also murdered . . ."

"Objection," cried Eileen O'Connor, jumping from her seat. "The charges against my client involve only three infants. No others."

"Objection sustained, but don't abuse the privilege, Ms. O'Connor. And Ms. Vasquez, please mind the rules," the judge warned. Opening statements were not to be interrupted unnecessarily, but prosecutors were also prohibited from referring to charges not in front of the jury. The judge continued, "Members of the jury, you will disregard the last statement made by the prosecutor." A small smile of victory crossed Vasquez's face. Even though the judge technically ruled against her, the damage was done. She had let the jury know that nine other infants were dead, and that bell couldn't be un-rung, despite the judge's admonishment.

"The state will present evidence that the defendant intentionally, willfully, and with malice aforethought, tampered with the healthy embryos in these three cases in such a way that the babies born from the embryos would eventually die horrible deaths from a genetic disease called Niemann-Pick."

For the record, she explained, she would be using the term "embryo" in a broad sense. Technically, when a sperm fertilizes an egg, the result is a one-celled organism called a zygote. That soon divides, becoming what's called a blastocyst, a collection of cells that can implant in the uterus. After several weeks, that becomes an embryo and a few weeks after that, a fetus.

The jurors stirred in their seats but looked straight at Vasquez.

Vasquez picked up on their discomfort and went on to explain that the case would be traumatic for the jury to hear. That the charge against the defendant was murder, plain and simple, nothing lesser, such as mere harm to an embryo or some sort of negligent homicide.

She added that she would present pictures of the deceased babies as their disease worsened, showing their tiny bellies, bloated despite their being unable to eat except through feeding tubes. And that she would be calling experts in the gene-editing technique called CRISPR, whose testimony might be hard to follow, but was crucial.

At the mention of the word "CRISPR," several members of the jury frowned. Vasquez rushed to reassure them.

"The state will make sure that this expert testimony is as clear and simple as possible. But I can give you the bottom line right now. This defendant inserted a lethal gene into the perfectly healthy DNA of these embryos knowing full well that the gene would give them the fatal disease Niemann-Pick."

She stood stock still, every eye upon her, the courtroom silent.

"The defendant is a murderer," she finished. "This defendant killed these innocent babies. Thank you."

The judge announced a fifteen-minute recess. Sammie rose, blew a kiss to Bob and the kids, and rushed to the small pressroom in the courthouse. She banged out two thousand words to get the copy desk started, hit the SEND button, then grabbed her purse and laptop and drove back to the *Times*.

2

SPRING 2018

Sammie had not always been one of the *Boston Times'* star reporters—far from it.

A mere two years ago, Sammie was a wet-behind-the-ears reporter at a paper in northern Massachusetts, the *Lowell Daily*, with a circulation of 50,000 and falling fast.

But it was a start, though the news staff was a motley group. The overweight reporter with the dirty hair who covered cops in Lowell and nearby Dracut had been there forever. Pushing sixty, she knew every cop in town, had slept with many of them, and carried a pearl-handled revolver in her purse.

The education reporter, a pleasant-bordering-on-passive man in his early forties, sat at the other adjoining desk, always on his cell, squeezing in a few work calls when he could between conversations with his bookie. The sports reporter, baseball cap on backward, muscular legs protruding from baggy shorts, never sat down. Instead, he patrolled the newsroom to talk Red Sox stats with anyone who dared look up from his or her computer.

And then there was Sammie, forty-one, the new kid in the newsroom, short and slight, with long dark hair. She wore eyeglasses, to appear older and more serious. The old-timers at the *Daily* called her "Ms. UC Berkeley," no matter how hard she tried to hide her fancy credentials. It had felt like a major breakthrough a few Fridays ago when they'd finally invited her for a beer after work. She had made it a quick one because the kids were home and Bob was on his way, but she finally, after three months on the job, started to feel included.

With a deadline approaching on this particular afternoon, Sammie twisted her hair into a hasty bun, inserting a pencil into the tangled mass to keep it all in place. If anyone had been looking, they'd have seen her squint at her computer screen, her brow wrinkled as she puzzled over the lede of her story for tomorrow's paper.

"The Chelmsford selectmen, with little debate, voted five to zero late yesterday afternoon to approve what until then had been a highly controversial . . ." Her lede sucked, but then again, she didn't have much to work with.

Her cell phone dinged. A text from Beau, her seven-year-old son. Liam, her ten-year-old, was into the Ben & Jerry's again, the text read, leaving none for Beau. Sammie called the boys at home.

"Guys, knock it off. I'll bring more ice cream when I get home. Liam, tell Beau you're sorry and don't eat anything else.

I'll be home in . . ." Sammie glanced at her watch, "an hour and a half. Put Maddy on."

Maddy was the seventeen-year-old, girl-next-door babysitter who watched the kids from three o'clock, when summer camp got out, until six o'clock, when either Sammie or Bob got home.

"Home" was a large condo in Cambridge that Sammie couldn't possibly have afforded without her parents' help. It wasn't fancy, but it was cozy and happily cluttered with books, newspapers, kids' sneakers, and all of the stuff they had moved in a year ago from Bob's bachelor pad.

Turkish rugs, "borrowed" from her parents, dressed the place up a bit, and Bob and Sammie had modernized the kitchen, installing a serious stove with six burners, so Bob could work his culinary magic.

"Maddy, try to keep the peace, honey. No more sweets for them. There are pretzels in the cupboard if they're starving. Thanks. See you," Sammie said, hanging up.

She turned back to her screen. Chelmsford. The town next to Lowell, Chelmsford was arguably the most boring municipality in the entire United States—34,000 suburbanites, all white, down to the picket fences protecting every tidy, identical lawn.

Chelmsford was the news-less beat no one else at the *Daily* would touch. Sammie had drawn the short straw because she was the newbie, having just discovered journalism after almost finishing her PhD in political science, teaching eighth grade, having kids, and slowly, very slowly, coming to terms with her husband Brad's death eight years ago.

"What," Sammie fought to remember, "was it that the selectmen had voted on this afternoon?" She flipped through her notes. "Ah, yes. Another thriller." She picked up her sentence . . . "discussion of what the town considered 'excessive flag display.' The issue arose last week when a business owner studded the area in front of his stationery store with dozens of American flags, angering residents and shoppers who said they felt emotionally assaulted by what they called 'excessive patriotism.'"

She sighed and slumped back. In the old days, she might have smoked, but Sammie had learned to avoid that trap, and as the five o'clock deadline approached, she reached for a new pack of gum, her second of the day. She started typing again, rushing to finish this story, climb into her trusty nondescript Camry, and get home by six o'clock.

Joe Green, the bearded night editor, strolled over, resting his hand on her shoulder, and peered closer to see her screen.

"How goes it, darlin'?" he asked. "Page One worthy?"

"Joseph, take your hand off my shoulder and don't call me 'darling.'" She went through this every night. He'd just separated from wife number three.

Sammie looked at him. "This story sucks. When can I start covering the Lowell city council instead of these Chelmsford bozos?"

"You have it good, darl . . ." he stopped himself. "When I covered Chelmsford, the selectmen, and I do mean select*men*, all wore plaid pants, white bucks, and smoked cigars. And I'm not kidding."

"These guys must have settled this stupid flag issue before the meeting. Nobody else was even in the room, except for a few ladies with their knitting," Sammie complained.

"You're the Fourth Estate, kid. The nation's watchdog. That counts," he said, heading to the city desk. "Hit the damn SEND button."

She typed a few more paragraphs, then sent him her story.

"Call me at home if the copy desk has any questions," Sammie called over to him. She pushed back from her chair, slung her purse over her shoulder, and headed for the door.

DINNER WAS THE usual exercise in controlled chaos. Bob was already home, God bless him, had made the salad and was just taking a luscious-smelling leftover mushroom and spinach lasagna out of the oven. Its seductive fragrance welcomed her as she came in the door. She quickly hung her jacket on the closet doorknob, kicked off her clogs, dumped her stuff in the hall, and headed for the kitchen.

Bob Brightman, a senior research associate at one of MIT's frontline genetics labs, had met Sammie on Match.com. Neither of them had expected much before they met, but they ended up having a whirlwind affair. Bob was in his late forties, never married, commitment-phobic. He also sang in one of Boston's best audition-only choruses and had filled the condo with classical music.

Bob was a whiz kid from Omaha with six siblings, a dentist father, and a chemist mother. The brothers, he had told her on their first date, had always been inventive. The Brightman boys made their own fun, including building a glider one summer and getting their youngest sister to jump off the garage roof in it, later explaining to their parents that she was the lightest, and therefore, the most likely to bounce.

For her part, Sammie had never expected to fall in love again. But after a few companionable jogs around nearby Fresh Pond with Bob, and a few romantic dinners in Harvard Square restaurants, Sammie had stashed the kids at their friends' houses and invited Bob to spend the night. Six months later, he moved in.

SAMMIE ENTERED THE warm kitchen, a bright yellow she had painted herself. She kissed Bob, probably a little too long, on the lips, snuggled in close for a moment, then went to the cupboard to get out the plates.

The boys, their faces still red and grubby from skateboarding all afternoon, dug in eagerly to the lasagna. Bob ate slowly, uncharacteristically silent. He was a talker, but not tonight. After Liam and Beau had finished and begun to torture each other, Sammie sent them off with the promise of more ice cream later.

"I got contacted by the medical examiner on an unusual case today," Bob began as soon as they were alone. He topped up his Sancerre. Sammie sipped hers and listened.

"A dead baby, about a year old. Totally weird. No signs of abuse or anything, just a baby, dead. A few skin lesions, a swollen belly. Just dead, for no clear reason."

"You don't usually get called in for something like this," Sammie said.

"No, but the M.E. seemed really stumped. He doesn't usually go with his gut, but he said his instinct told him something was really wrong in this case."

Sammie stopped eating. They say that the hair on the back of a person's neck stands up at the first sign of danger. Her neck hairs weren't twitching, but her journalistic instincts were. She'd learned to trust that.

"Are you going to work with him?" she asked.

"We'll see."

As Bob washed dishes, Sammie saw to baths and clean jammies, fixed herself some hibiscus tea, and nestled next to Beau in his bed. He curled up next to her under his favorite Spiderman sheets as she glanced over to Liam in the nearby twin bed. Liam was glued to his beloved Percy Jackson book, *The Lightning Thief,* but looked over and smiled at Beau and her.

Last week, Beau had surprised her by getting weepy at bedtime. He'd wanted to talk about his father. "How come Liam got to see him and I didn't?" he'd asked.

"Oh, sweetheart," she'd said, putting down the book she was reading him. "Would you like to hear the story again?"

"Yeah," he'd said.

"Liam, wanna come over here for a snuggle? You can help tell the story." Liam had crawled into Beau's bed on her other side.

"Now we're a Mom sandwich," Beau had said happily.

And she'd told the story, from the beginning. How she'd met Brad Fuller in college, at UC Berkeley freshman year and how they had become inseparable. How in the fall of their senior year, they'd gotten engaged. They'd been married ten years when they'd had Liam.

When Liam was still an infant, Brad was diagnosed with an aggressive form of melanoma. Anticipating years of chemotherapy and radiation, they'd frozen Brad's sperm.

About two years after Brad died, Sammie decided to get pregnant again, and along came Beau.

3

SPRING 2018

The next morning at work, Sammie had just refilled her coffee and sorted through her emails, when she got a text from Bob.

"Call me," it said, followed by three hearts.

"What's up?" she asked when he picked up. She waved off the city editor who was approaching, flipping through his notebook of what were sure to be awful story ideas.

"I just talked to the M.E. again," Bob said. "I'm sure I sounded like a total asshole, but I'm too busy to help him now." She could hear the guilt in his voice, but it was just one baby dead of unknown causes. That probably happened all the time.

Sammie could hardly blame him. It wasn't his job to solve puzzling autopsy cases.

Then it hit her. Mother's Day was coming up. She wondered aloud if the mother of this poor baby might want to tell her story, if for no other reason than to remind harried, stressed-out mothers how precious their children were, how lucky they were to have healthy, living children. It would be a lot to ask of a grieving mother, but people in distress sometimes wanted to tell their stories.

"Go for it, babe," said Bob, after she suggested that to him. "I'll see if the M.E. will give me the mother's name." He fell silent. "He did tell me the baby was conceived through IVF. That's got to be extra heartbreaking, to go through all that, then have the baby die."

Sammie told him she loved him, thanked him, and hung up. She faked a smile at the approaching city editor. The surefire way to dodge his dumb ideas was to parry with a good one of her own.

THE NEXT AFTERNOON, Sammie settled into a corner table at Au Bon Pain in Harvard Square with Josie Reimann Northrup. Josie took her coffee black. Sammie liked hers with the works. She bought a couple of still-warm chocolate chip cookies, too. Josie smiled weakly as Sammie sat down on the ugly plastic chair.

Josie's eyes were red-rimmed, her face pale and worn, but she was a pretty woman. She didn't know how much Josie used to weigh, but she looked skeletal now. Her stylish Newbury Street haircut was growing out. She wore no eye makeup.

"I'm so sorry about your baby," Sammie began, keeping her notebook and digital recorder in her purse for the moment. To put

Josie at ease, Sammie told her a bit about herself, her early widow-hood, her meeting Bob, her frustrations with the *Lowell Daily*, her eagerness to get to a big paper like the *Boston Times*. Sammie tried to downplay her life as a mother, but she did say that she had two boys and couldn't imagine losing either one of them.

"I had a boy, too," Josie said softly. "Jamie."

Sammie held her gaze, then took out her notebook and recorder. She raised her eyebrows. Josie nodded. With the silent approval, Sammie began recording.

In between sips of coffee, Josie told Sammie that she had been a college rower, which Sammie could believe, pegging Josie's height at about five feet nine. Despite her current thin-ness, she was fit.

Until recently, Josie told her, she had thought of herself as incredibly lucky, a golden girl. Her parents, both academics, were Brits from northern Yorkshire, who were on sabbatical in Kenya when Josie was born.

She had loved Africa. Thanks to her native governesses and babysitters, she became fluent in Kikuyu and Swahili. She told Sammie that when her parents moved back to England and then on to Pennsylvania, she took pride in telling her class-mates that she was African.

For a moment, she almost seemed to shed her grief as she recounted going on to Penn on a full scholarship. At Penn, she met her future husband, Peter Northrup, in a freshman psychol-ogy class. She ended up majoring in psych because she wanted to be a therapist. She paid for grad school by modeling.

She actually laughed when she looked at Sammie and said, "I knew modeling agencies would love me for a few years after college, but I also knew they'd dump me at the first sign of wrinkles or any extra pounds."

She fell silent then, grief reasserting itself. Her shoulders slumped, her chin dropped. Sammie waited.

"Another cookie?" Sammie finally ventured. Josie shook her head.

Clutching her Kleenex, Josie described her life with Peter, including her booming psychotherapy business and Peter's long hours as a partner in his small law firm.

But the last couple of years had been hell. Month after month, with her fortieth birthday approaching and no pregnancy yet, sex had become joyless, a grim duty to be accomplished at specific times of the month. She had begun taking her basal temperature obsessively to see if it had gone up, a signal of possible ovulation. If it did, they would make love immediately, mechanically. Several times, when Josie took her temperature in her office between patients, she and Peter would rush home, make love, shower fast, then rush back to work.

Tears of frustration filled her eyes. Sammie's eyes got misty, too. Teenagers, Josie went on bitterly, could get pregnant in the back seats of cars in thirty seconds. And here she and Peter were young, healthy, with a stable marriage and a decent bank account, and they couldn't manage life's most basic task: reproducing.

"Mother Nature didn't really set things up in my favor," she went on. "Maybe for you," she looked at Sammie, "since you had kids early. But for me? We're supposed to be born with, what, one million eggs? I've lost most of them by now."

Sammie nodded and waited for Josie to resume.

"Still, how many eggs does it take to make a baby? Just one, right? But there are only twelve months in the year, a lousy twelve chances to get pregnant." Sammie's stomach clenched.

She had never really thought about how easily she'd gotten pregnant or how awful it would be if she hadn't been able to.

Josie took a sip of her lukewarm coffee, then continued. She had started taking Clomid, the ovary-stimulating drug. She'd bought commercial pee tests that were supposed to predict exactly when she would ovulate, and she had tried them all—Clear Blue, First Response, and Knowhen.

The turning point, she went on, had been a heart-to-heart talk with her best friend, Ashlyn, at their favorite Cambridge bar, Christopher's.

"You should meet Ashlyn Wilson," she told Sammie, her face briefly animated again. "You'd like her. She's thirty-nine." Ashlyn, Josie continued, was a molecular biologist, a malaria researcher, single, and desperate to have a child on her own. The two friends decided then and there to do IVF together at the same clinic. Josie had gone home that night and told Peter about the idea. He wasn't wild about it, but he had agreed.

IVF had been a nightmare. Josie and Peter had liked Dr. Saul Kramer, the head of the clinic. But emotionally, the process had been relentless. Endless blood tests, ultrasounds, and nightly injections of hormones and other drugs that had made her even more depressed than she already was.

One of the worst experiences had been the hysterosalpingogram.

"I didn't care what it was called," she recounted. "I just wanted it over with." Sammie couldn't blame her.

Dr. Kramer had explained that he had to look at her uterus, ovaries, and fallopian tubes to make sure the tubes were open, that there was no scarring or anything in her uterus, and that her ovaries looked healthy. The good thing was that she had been able to look at a monitor on a nearby stand to see the

X-ray images as the procedure unfolded. She remembered squealing as Kramer inserted the catheter through her vagina into her uterus, and then being fascinated as her eyes followed the blue dye as it squirted from the catheter into her uterus, then up through her fallopian tubes.

Then, agony. She remembered screaming: "Something's wrong!" Just cramps, Dr. Kramer had reassured her. And he'd had good news. Her tubes were open and her uterus looked good, totally normal. He had slowly withdrawn the catheter, then had done a quick ultrasound probe through her vagina to check out her ovaries. Again, everything looked good.

After that, there were weeks of ovarian stimulation, with hormone injections that Peter did until she eventually learned to do them herself. She'd endured the "mock embryo transfer," which, if anything, had triggered worse cramps than the hysterosalpingogram. She had ended up in tears.

Then, finally, the process of surgically "harvesting" the few viable eggs Josie had managed to produce, and the injection of Peter's sperm into the eggs.

She paused in her tale, and Sammie felt guilty about asking her to relive it all. But Josie gamely continued, recounting how thrilled they were when they found out that she was pregnant. Josie actually smiled at the memory. Sammie didn't dare smile, knowing the tragedy ahead.

"The actual birth was horrible," Josie admitted.

Sammie shuddered, remembering Liam's birth with Brad at her side, and little Beau's, all on her own.

Josie explained that Peter had later told her that her screams echoed down the hospital corridor, but during the process, all he did was tell her how great she was doing, how much he loved her, and how it was almost over.

"He could not have been more supportive," she added.

Ashlyn, by then pregnant with her own baby, had been allowed in the delivery room too, and had held Josie's other hand. The best friends had promised that, if they survived the IVF process, they would be there for each other's deliveries.

And then the tiny head had emerged, thin hair wet and matted, cupped in the midwife's gloved hands. A final push and then Peter's voice, "We have a son!"

"I had never seen him so happy," Josie smiled. "Ashlyn was crying with joy, too." When the midwife had bundled the baby in a blue flannel blanket and placed him on her chest, she went on, she had felt a tsunami of love.

"I had never felt anything like that in my entire life, this wave of bliss, of sacredness."

Sammie stopped breathing. She was always awed when women described the moment of a child's birth.

Josie and Peter had had a long list of names, but when the baby had finally arrived, Peter had looked at Josie, letting her decide.

"James," Josie had said. "James Reimann Northrup. Jamie." Peter had stroked his son's impossibly soft cheek as Josie watched his chest swell with pride.

Josie suddenly stopped talking. She stared at her coffee, the liquid now as cold as her voice. Sammie waited until Josie collected herself enough to go on with her tale.

For the first six or seven months, Josie said, her voice growing quieter, Jamie had seemed fine. He cooed and gurgled, nursed well, and locked eyes with Josie in that wonderful thing psychologists called the "mutual gaze."

Josie and Peter, of course, had been over the moon, both taking parental leave—Josie, three months totally off work,

Peter, cutting back to half time—and they practically fought for the privilege of changing and bathing him. Peter snapped picture after picture on his phone, deluging their friends and family with dozens of photos a day. Nobody had the heart to ask him to send fewer pictures. Everybody knew how hard they had tried to get this baby.

Then, as Jamie approached his first birthday, light brown spots began appearing all over his skin, and freckles in his armpits and groin area.

"Café au lait spots," said the first pediatrician. Josie and Peter had looked at one another, mystified. Did birthmarks just appear? Like freckles brought out by the sun? The doctor had explained that the spots had nothing to do with the sun. It was most likely a disease called neurofibromatosis type 1.

"Neuro *what*?" Josie had exploded just as Peter blurted out, "Will he die?"

No, the pediatrician had assured them. It was probably just a random mutation and Jamie would almost certainly go on to live a normal life. Over the years, he might develop some non-cancerous tumors on his nerves, but these could be surgically removed if necessary.

Not exactly reassured, Josie and Peter had taken Jamie to Boston's Children's Hospital. Again, a pediatrician tried to calm their fears. Yes, it was probably neurofibromatosis type 1, she said. He had been born with it. It was not their fault, most likely some random mutation.

The pediatrician assured them that most children born with this condition lived normal life spans. The biggest problem, she added, would probably be the child's anxiety about the spots when he became a teenager. He might also have high blood pressure in later life, but that, too, should be manageable.

They had tried to pretend Jamie was normal, but as he approached his first birthday his belly began swelling and he had trouble swallowing. The growing list of symptoms no longer matched his diagnosis of neurofibromatosis, but the doctors had had no answers. They didn't know why the disease seemed to be taking an uncharted course.

As Sammie listened intently, Josie went on to describe how, during the final months of Jamie's illness, they had hired a nurse to stay with him during the few hours a week that Josie could tear herself away to see her most severely troubled patients in her office. Thankfully, she was also able to do some telephone therapy from home with a few others.

At first, she hadn't told her patients what was going on in her own life, but, as Jamie's condition worsened, she knew she had no choice. Most of her patients were sympathetic, but their sympathy, not surprisingly, ended up complicating their therapy. They felt guilty talking about their own problems, knowing about Josie's. Several had reluctantly quit and gone to other therapists, but Josie hadn't had the emotional space to worry about that. Losing her work, her hard-earned practice, patient by patient, was nothing compared to the prospect of losing her baby.

At that point, she had mostly stayed home with Jamie, holding her sick child in her arms for hours at a time, staring into his face while he slept, desperately willing her own life force into his failing body. Eventually, Peter would pry the baby away and hold Jamie while Josie collapsed into restless sleep.

Peter hadn't fared much better. He had worked at home as much as he could, except when he had to be in court to argue a case. His colleagues at the law firm cut him some slack, for which he was always grateful. How could they not, watching as his suits hung ever more loosely on his once-sturdy frame as he became a shell of the man he once was? He was grateful for their support, but not being physically at the office gnawed at him. How could he hold his own if he wasn't there for daily meetings?

"And now, our Jamie is gone. Dead. We had him for just one year." Sadness had etched deep lines in Josie's face.

There was nothing Sammie could say. She touched Josie gently on her arm, quietly clicked off her digital recorder, and put away her notebook. This was not just another story. This was life itself.

"I don't have to write this, you know," Sammie finally said softly. "You're not obligated to share this with the world."

Josie sat up straighter than she had all afternoon.

"I want to. And there's one other thing I'd like."

Sammie waited.

"We haven't had the memorial service yet for Jamie. We were waiting until after the autopsy. But it's next week. I'd be honored if you would come."

4

SPRING 2018

The Unitarian Universalist church in Harvard Square was packed.

The unbearably tiny coffin sat at the front, barely visible amid all the flowers. A poster-sized photograph of Jamie, at six months old, was propped up on an easel for all to see. The child's face was still beautiful, still normal-looking, the eyes wide open, trusting. Sammie couldn't take her eyes off that innocent face, yet found she had to keep looking away and eventually just rested her head on Bob's shoulder.

Josie sat numb and dry-eyed in the front row, holding hands tightly on one side with Ashlyn, whose own baby, Katy, now six months old, was at home with a babysitter, and Peter on the other. Josie's mother sat nearby.

The mere thought, let alone the reality, of losing a child was unbearable. Even from her seat a few rows back, Sammie could see Josie's body trembling, her shoulders and Ashlyn's shaking almost in unison. Sammie was not religious, but today she prayed for all she was worth, for Josie, for Peter, for little Jamie, and for her own precious boys.

Josie's mother was still, as still as death. Her father sat slumped with his elbows on his knees, his head hanging low, his shoulders shaking with silent sobs. Josie was their only child, and Jamie their only grandchild. Josie's father's grief was not just for his daughter's unimaginable suffering, but for the loss of the family's legacy, the loss of hope that, through Jamie, the Reimann family would continue into the future.

Every single one of the women from Josie's IVF group was sitting in the second row, frozen in place. Starting with Kramer's first introductory seminar, the women had bonded tightly. They had gone through the hell of IVF procedures together, all determined to fulfill that deep biological need to have a child. During those endless months, they had texted each other often, offering their support, sharing questions, and increasingly joy, as conceptions occurred and real, live babies were born. They had met in person as often as they could, taking turns hosting. Now, they were all new mothers, just as Josie had been. Unlike Josie, most of their babies were still just a few months old. They empathized with Josie's loss, but that very empathy felt terrifying, like tempting fate. What had happened to Josie's baby? What might happen to theirs?

Behind the first two rows were several hundred of Josie's psychotherapy colleagues, friends, and acquaintances from college and grad school days. Even a few friends from Josie's hometown in Pennsylvania were there, clutching tissues, dabbing their eyes and whispering the same words over and over to each other: "I can't believe it," "I can't imagine what Josie is going through," "This is beyond unfair."

At the front, the minister, a young black woman dressed simply in black pants and blouse, with a purple shawl around her shoulders, waited, composed, as the organist played Bach's "Sheep May Safely Graze." The familiar tune sounded different today, so *espressivo*, every note infused with sorrow.

At the back of the church, a man sat with his wife, her arm tucked under his. He had the look of a scientist whose mind was elsewhere. He allowed his eyes to close.

IT MUST HAVE been more than a decade ago now. He had accepted a new patient at his Boston-area IVF clinic, Elisabeth Seidl Mannheim, who had come into his office in tears with her husband, Josef Mannheim.

They had been trying for more than a year to get pregnant, said Elisabeth, who asked him to call her "Lisbett," her voice quavering as she mopped her eyes with a tissue. Josef, dry-eyed but pale, said nothing, barely making eye contact.

He had dutifully explained the IVF procedures, which the desperate couple had followed religiously. After several months, she had produced three eggs, which he had fertilized in the lab with Josef's sperm. But one day, as he peered into the microscope to do his usual preimplantation screening to make sure the eggs were healthy and the chromosomes were all there and intact, he froze.

"Seidl, Seidl, Seidl," he mused. Why was that name, Lisbett's maiden name, so familiar? He was sure he had had no other patients by that name, nor any friends, either. His mind whirring, he sat down and leaned forward in his chair, elbows on his thighs, his face held up by his hands, Lisbett's fertilized eggs waiting on his lab counter.

Suddenly, he knew. In high school, he had become obsessed with the Nazis, in particular the Nuremburg trials and the concentration camps.

In the first trial, the International Military Tribunal—described by one of the judges as "the greatest trial in history"—twenty-four of the worst of the Nazis were tried. Twelve were sentenced to death, seven went to prison, three were acquitted and two ended up not charged.

For several years, he had pored over the Nuremburg literature, set on becoming a lawyer, hoping to model himself on the heroic prosecutors of the Nazis. The law, in his teenage mind, would be the best way to achieve justice. Though that ambition would later fade as he excelled in his science courses and began thinking about medicine, he never lost his thirst for justice.

His obsessive reading eventually took him to documented stories about one camp in particular, Theresienstadt. This was the camp his mother had spoken of. The way she spat the word, he'd heard its echo in his head all his life. He was surprised to learn that Theresienstadt was considered not just a concentration camp but a kind of "camp-ghetto" and transit station from which Jews were sent to extermination camps.

The chain of command at the camp was clear. At the top was SS First Lieutenant Siegfried Seidl, who ran the place. He reported to a man named Gunther, who in turn reported directly to Adolf Eichmann in Berlin. Seidl was in charge from November 24, 1941, until July 3, 1943. After the war, he was tried, found guilty, and executed.

All these years later, that name had rung a bell for the man. Could Lisbett, the former Ms. Seidl, be a direct descendant of Seidl, the Nazi commander?

The doctor-scientist had stood up and peered through the microscope again. Was there Nazi DNA in these hard-won eggs? There was, of course, no gene for Nazism, but the Nazi commander's DNA could quite plausibly be in the DNA of this desperate, innocent woman.

Before he had time to think about what he was doing, he took the slide with Lisbett's eggs on it, grabbed a flask of alcohol, and poured it over the eggs. A breakdown product of the alcohol, acetaldehyde, was well-known as a toxin that can damage DNA. He tossed the wet slide into the hazardous medical waste pail and took off his gloves.

The couple would be devastated, of course. But the doctor's face was relaxed as he finished cleaning up the lab. His shoulders were a good inch lower than earlier in the day. It was a minor act of revenge. *No,* he thought, *not revenge, justice. The couple could get pregnant again on the next cycle. No harm done.* And that's just what had happened. The next cycle was a good one, the eggs fertilized easily and after a brief moment of doubt, he had implanted the fertilized eggs successfully in Lisbett's womb.

BACK IN THE church, the last chords were dying away. The minister began, her eyes meeting Josie's with compassion.

"There is no way to understand the death of Jamie Reimann Northrup," the minister began. "There is no way that a benevolent God would ever intend this. This is not God's will. God is crying with us today."

The mourners gave up trying to hold back their tears as the minister continued. "As I thought about what to say today, what words could possibly help comfort Josie, Peter, Josie's mother and father, and Peter's parents, and all of you, Josie's friends and family, I thought of the words of poet Mary Oliver. Let me read them to you now."

The minister read slowly: "To live in this world, you must be able to do three things: to love what is mortal; to hold it against your bones knowing your own life depends on it; and, when the time comes to let it go, to let it go."

The poet's words unleashed a chorus of sobs from the congregation. The service went solemnly on, with sad hymns, words of solace and support from friends, and testimonials to Josie's courage.

When the service ended, Josie, Peter, and her parents rode together back home. The IVF support group set off right away, too, to lay out cold cuts, cheeses, fruit, sourdough bread, cupcakes, and cookies, and have the coffee ready so that its aroma would perfume the hallway to welcome people in the best way they knew how.

Bob and Sammie stayed behind. Sammie had noticed a dignified-looking man standing awkwardly at the back of the church with an overdressed, tightly coiffed woman, presumably his wife, at his side. Sammie walked toward them, going on instinct.

"Dr. Saul Kramer?" Sammie offered her hand. He nodded and took it.

"Yes. How did you know?"

"I didn't. But Josie has spoken kindly of you and I thought you might come."

"But, of course," he answered, introducing his wife, Ellen, as Sammie introduced Bob.

The silence that followed was awkward.

"It must be so sad for you," Sammie began. "Helping a couple get pregnant, then losing the baby."

"It is, of course it is," he answered. "It rarely happens, but when it does . . ." His voice trailed off. It was nothing Sammie could put her finger on, but was there something in his face, or maybe in his eyes, or maybe in his voice? Was Sammie imagining things, or had his wife sensed something, too?

"Saul," his wife said, threading her arm through his, then turning to Sammie. "You have to understand. He has helped so many couples get pregnant." Losing a baby he had helped create, she went on, was incredibly difficult for him. "He gets choked up. This is almost as hard on him as on the couple."

Sammie doubted that. She cast Bob a sideways look. He understood the implied question, nodding back almost imperceptibly.

Sammie turned back to Kramer.

"Dr. Kramer, I'm a reporter, for the *Lowell Daily*." She explained that she was working on a story about Josie for Mother's Day. Even though it was terribly sad, she said, it had piqued her interest in IVF. Sammie was flattering him, of course, but her curiosity about IVF was real.

He cocked his head. Sammie plunged on.

"I'd like to do a story on IVF, how it works, how often it results in a baby, all that. Could I possibly come interview you and see your clinic?"

Sammie thought she just saw him pale ever so slightly. He recovered quickly.

"Of course," he said smiling, though his eyes didn't crinkle. "Set it up with my secretary."

They mumbled a few more pleasantries, then said their goodbyes. The Kramers headed for their Lexus; Bob and Sammie to her Camry.

AT JOSIE AND Peter's, bottles of wine and rows of glasses stood lined up on the kitchen island, along with a bottle of Jameson's.

Josie came over to greet Sammie and Bob, then silently slipped away. Peter offered them wine or whiskey. They gratefully chose the latter. Several of the women also asked for whiskey, as did Josie's father. Peter grabbed more whiskey glasses from the cabinet and handed generous pours all around. The guests mingled quietly.

Josie's friends from the IVF group commandeered the couch, squeezing together when suddenly, from across the room, came an unearthly sound.

Josie had been standing near her mother against the wall, then had slowly slid down and crumpled on the floor, wailing. It was a sound so haunting, so primitive, that everyone froze, glasses raised midair, partway to lips, hands frozen as they reached for nibbles. The entire room looked as if its occupants were playing the children's game of statues.

The sound was penetrating, not so much in volume as in intensity. It came from somewhere deep and primal. Josie could not stop, and no one asked her to. Peter walked silently over to her, sank to his knees, and embraced her. His own eyes now streaming, he whispered in her ear.

His body collapsed onto hers, his sobs punctuating her cries.

Josie's mother stepped away from the grieving couple and went to the bedroom—the pain too unbearable for a mother to watch. Josie's father walked to the kitchen, refilled his whiskey, then sank into an easy chair, with a blank look on his face.

Finally, Josie looked up, her eyes locking for a moment with Ashlyn's, then with each woman from the IVF group in turn. "I took Jamie to three different pediatricians," she said. "I even took him to a pediatric oncologist to see if maybe he had cancer. Why could no one help him? I just don't understand."

Nobody did. There was nothing to say. After a while, the guests began to slip out. Josie's IVF friends apologized profusely, saying that they had to go. They didn't need to say why they had to leave—everyone knew they still had their babies to feed.

Sammie caught Bob's eye. They should leave, too. Sammie was flooded, suddenly, with guilt and gratitude. Her children were still alive. There were bedtime stories to read.

ASHLYN WAS THE last to leave, torn between getting home to her sweet baby, Katy, and staying longer with Josie and Peter. Finally, she drove home slowly, filled with a heaviness she had never felt before. She methodically stashed her jacket in the closet, set her purse down on the coffee table, paid the babysitter, and collapsed on the couch holding her precious Katy. The innocent little face that looked back at her was beautiful—big blue eyes, button nose, and chubby cheeks, all framed by wispy, blonde curls.

But as Katy's eyes closed, Ashlyn sank farther back on the couch, her child's soft weight warming her chest.

Her thoughts turned dark again. Was Katy really okay? She looked fine. Unlike Jamie, little Katy had no weird skin spots. But the pediatrician had seemed puzzled at the visit last week. Katy's liver and spleen had been slightly enlarged. And she had had a few pea-sized bumps under the skin. Ashlyn knew that Jamie had been diagnosed with neurofibromatosis, but the pediatrician didn't think Katy had that.

"Has she been eating well?" the doctor had asked.

"Not always," Ashlyn had admitted. "Sometimes she seems to have a stomachache."

"Hmmm," mused the doctor. Then, in a more professional voice, he added, "I'd like you to bring her back in a week or so. I'd like to see her again. I'm not quite sure what's going on."

5

EARLY SUMMER 2018

The IVF clinic was dazzling in the afternoon sun. The modern building had glass everywhere, decks with overflowing flower boxes, landscaped parking area, picnic tables under maple trees in the back, a volleyball court in the side yard, a weeping willow on the bank of a stream.

Sammie pressed the buzzer. A young female voice answered, "We're expecting you, Ms. Fuller." The door clicked and Sammie walked in, glancing up at the light pouring in from the large skylights above.

Dr. Saul Kramer himself strode out to meet her, an alpha male, clearly the master of his territory, a far cry from the ill-at-ease man Sammie had met at the church. He wore a casual sport jacket, no tie, and a shirt open at the neck. No need for a white coat to scream authority; Kramer's was unmistakable.

He was a pleasantly paunchy, round-faced sixty-year-old, with an impressive head of white hair and a well-earned reputation among his colleagues for his brilliance, and among his patients for his kindness. He was one of the superstar docs populating Boston's world-class hospitals, including this sprawling fertility clinic twenty miles west of the city where, for years, infertile couples had flocked in desperation.

It didn't take a genius to see that Kramer was pure "Preparation H"—Harvard undergrad (Phi Beta Kappa, of course) and Harvard Med. Before Harvard, he had gone to the elite Boston Latin School. After Harvard Med, he had received a PhD from MIT in genetics and reproductive endocrinology.

"Come in, come in," he said, offering his hand. Behind him, a solemn-faced couple was just emerging from his office, clutching papers and looking lost.

"Please sit over there in the waiting room," Kramer said, turning to them. "You can read the handouts while you wait." He added that the seminar would start in a few minutes and that his secretary could get them coffee or soft drinks, if they'd like.

"Follow me, Ms. Fuller," he said, nodding to her and turning back toward his office.

"Please, it's Samantha," Sammie said, following him.

He settled himself behind his massive mahogany desk. Sammie took a chair opposite him and stared at the walls plastered with photos of babies and beaming parents, handwritten notes of gratitude, and numerous framed diplomas, plaques, and awards from professional societies. Sammie was impressed, despite herself.

On the corner of his desk sat an eight-by-ten silver frame holding a picture of a baby. The child looked serious in that innocent way babies have when they are calmly looking out at the world.

"Your child?" Sammie asked.

"Isaiah," he nodded solemnly. "He died a long time ago."

"I'm so sorry," Sammie said. "That's awful."

Kramer fell silent, staring at his lap. Sammie felt a wave of sadness and studied Kramer's face. She consciously stilled herself, for once not rushing to interrupt, and simply sat with him.

FORGETTING HIS GUEST and even his surroundings, Kramer closed his eyes, lost as he had been so many times before, recalling that night twenty years ago. It was after dinner. He and Ellen were watching the news together on TV. Saul had then retired to his study, while Ellen cleaned up.

Like his desk at work, his home desk was cluttered with various genetics journals—he had some subscriptions sent to his office and others to his home. He had allowed himself a few frivolous minutes to browse the more far-out stuff. He had sighed and moved the pile of journals slightly to reveal the photograph of his last-born son, Isaiah. The same picture he had a copy of in his office.

Taken when Isaiah was four months old, the baby face that gazed back at him looked almost normal to a doting father's eye.

But to a geneticist like Saul, the picture also showed hints of what was to come: Niemann-Pick disease, the scourge of Ashkenazi Jews that kills innocent, beautiful babies in infancy.

Before Isaiah was born, neither Saul nor Ellen had any reason to suspect that they might be carriers of Niemann-Pick.

Nobody on either side of their families had had the disease, at least as far as they knew. Their first three children, now adults, appeared normal, though they would later learn that all three were carriers of the disease.

But, as Isaiah's situation led them to discover to their dismay, their seemingly healthy family track record had been pure luck. Apparently, their parents and grandparents had all married partners with healthy genes, so none of their offspring had the disease. But their own parents had been carriers, and both had passed the deadly mutation to Saul and Ellen. That meant a 25 percent chance with each of Ellen's pregnancies that the baby would inherit the deadly, autosomal recessive Niemann-Pick gene.

Isaiah, poor thing, was that one in four chance. He inherited two copies of the bad mutation, one from Ellen, one from Saul. In his short, tragic life, the bad mutation would trigger a riot of problems, most notably the failure of his body to properly break down fats like oils and cholesterol, which then accumulated in his brain, muscles, lungs, bone marrow, and elsewhere.

It had been the most horrifying experience—watching their infant son turn, in a matter of a few short months, from the latest blessing of their lives into a baby who could no longer swallow, whose eyes crossed, whose muscles turned stiff and spastic, whose lymph nodes swelled up, and whose belly bloated as his liver and spleen became enlarged. When Isaiah's eyes turned cloudy, Saul had shined a light into them. What he saw was a cherry-red halo in the center of Isaiah's retinas. The hallmark of Niemann-Pick, Type A, the worst type.

When he saw that cherry-red sign, Saul had dropped his penlight and collapsed on the floor in sobs, clutching little

Isaiah tightly to his chest. Ellen, hearing him fall, had rushed in from the living room.

"What happened?" she cried, seeing her husband and baby huddled on the floor.

Saul couldn't speak. Ellen dropped to her knees and lay down next to Saul. She pulled both husband and baby to her chest and held tight.

"Tell me, tell me," she begged. "I can't stand it."

Saul couldn't form the dreaded words.

"It's, it's . . . Niemann-Pick," he finally managed.

"What's that? I never heard of it," Ellen whispered. "Is it bad? Is he going to die?"

Saul could not meet his wife's eyes. Agony feeding fury, she roughly tilted his chin up and thrust her face into his, noses almost touching.

"Saul, you have to tell me."

He paused, slowly raising his eyes to look into hers.

"Yes, it's bad. It's very bad. Very, very bad. He is going to die. I doubt he'll live much past his first birthday."

"Oh, my God. Is it my fault?" asked Ellen. "What did we do wrong?"

"Nothing, honey, nothing. It's genetic," he replied as soothingly as he could.

They fell silent. Isaiah snuggled between them.

The child coughed, and Saul and Ellen moved apart to give him air. With Ellen holding Isaiah, they crawled a few feet to lean back against the sofa.

"You are *not* going to die, my sweet little one," Ellen spoke sternly to Isaiah. Tears streamed down her face, landing on Isaiah's chest. "I won't let you. I will not let this happen."

Saul said nothing, but leaned his head on her shoulder and encircled his little family with his arm, completing the pietà.

Isaiah died an excruciating eight months later.

KRAMER SEEMED TO emerge suddenly from his rumination, remembering with a jerk that he was in his office. He looked at Sammie for a moment, looked away, avoiding her eyes, then sat up straighter and turned to her.

"Where was I?" he mumbled.

"You were going to explain IVF," Sammie said kindly, digging out her digital recorder and notebook. "Do you mind if I record this?"

"Not at all," he said, reaching into his top drawer and slapping his own recorder on the table. "So long as you don't mind if I record it, too. If I'm going to be quoted in your newspaper, I want to be sure you get it right."

It was a reasonable request, of course. But it was aggressive, too. Sammie bristled, but returned his serve with a smile. "I get things right, Dr. Kramer. It's a point of honor with me."

"Good," he said, then paused. "So, what do you want to know?"

"What you do here."

Mostly, he explained, he and his staff tried to help infertile couples get pregnant. Sometimes it worked. Sometimes it didn't. They also, he went on, were heavily invested in research with CRISPR.

"With what?" Sammie interrupted. Interruption was an occupational hazard for journalists like her.

"CRISPR. The new gene-editing technique."

Ah. The word rang a dim bell. Bob had mentioned something about that and had seemed excited, but it was way over her head, so Sammie hadn't paid much attention, only absorbing a word here or there when he talked about it.

Kramer picked up on her confusion.

"Let's save that for later when I show you my lab. For now, let's start with IVF, the process, and what really goes on here."

An idea seemed to pop into his head. Would Sammie like, he wondered, to sit in on a seminar with new patients that—he glanced at his watch—was about to start? The patients would have to agree, of course. And Sammie would have to promise not to quote any of them, even anonymously, HIPAA regs and all that. But Sammie could get to hear about IVF and how it worked. He voiced the question and Sammie agreed, gathered her things, and followed him to the seminar room.

Sammie detected a slight smile as Kramer surveyed his patients. Eight women, a few with nervous-looking husbands, sat stiffly around the polished teak table. The coffee mugs, emblazoned with KRAMER RESEARCH LAB, were still steaming, mostly untouched, at each place, alongside new pads of lined notepaper and pens, also marked with Kramer's distinctive logo.

The women looked to be mostly in their forties, a few a little younger. One, with red hair and freckles, introduced herself as coming from a very fertile Irish family. Everybody laughed sympathetically as she explained that, unlike her five sisters, all of whom had gotten pregnant on their honeymoons, she had been unable to conceive after a year of marriage. Her husband, a silent, beefy guy, picked at his fingernails and jiggled his leg under the table as she talked.

The others, including two black women and one Asian woman, took turns telling of their desperate attempts to get pregnant as Kramer listened to the familiar tales. IVF was the last chance for these women. And they knew it.

When they were done with the introductions, he told them he was pleased at the ethnic diversity the clinic attracted, and the wide range of education and financial resources, as well. Sammie wondered briefly why diversity had anything to do with a fertility clinic, then let the thought go.

Kramer plunged into his speech, an act he had clearly mastered over the years, noting the grim fact that the birth rate for each cycle of IVF decreased the older a woman was. Sammie saw the Irish woman's husband squeeze her knee under the table. The black woman lost a bit of her bravado.

Kramer went on, explaining about sperm samples. Many, many sperm samples. The men squirmed each time the word "sperm" was mentioned.

"Now, ladies, your part," Kramer continued. He described the different protocols for the IVF process, including medications to stop premature ovulation. He explained that the goal was to suppress ovulation with birth control pills, then do daily injections of hormones to trigger tightly controlled ovulation and, hopefully, produce a lot more healthy eggs at that time.

After that, the woman would get a drug called hCG to finalize the egg maturation. Then he would keep the eggs safe until it was time to fertilize and implant them. Just before implanting the fertilized eggs, Kramer went on, he would do a preimplantation genetic screening to ensure that each one had the right number of chromosomes. The women were so busy scribbling notes they didn't notice the subtle change in Kramer's demeanor as he described this last step.

But Sammie did.

As THE GROUP filed silently out of the seminar room, Kramer removed the sports jacket he wore to put patients at ease and donned the crisp white lab coat with DR. SAUL KRAMER monogrammed in red above the pocket. His mood seemed to change as fast as his clothing. "Come along," he beckoned to Sammie. She hastily gathered her things once again and hustled to keep up with him as he strode down the hall to the Kramer Genetics Lab.

He nodded curtly to the fellows and research assistants at their workstations. It was clear he ran a tight ship. Sammie had heard that the competition to work with Kramer was fierce.

The younger scientists glanced at one another, then lowered their heads toward their computer screens. They had become adept at deciphering Kramer's moods. They knew his patients loved him, but the high turnover rate in the lab suggested that his scientific underlings felt otherwise.

Sammie looked around at the vast lab. Computers, centrifuges, refrigerators, who knew what else. She had visited Bob in his lab many times, but still didn't know what all the machines were for, or who did what, much less exactly why. She noticed security cameras, too, all mounted high on the walls near the ceiling.

She glanced over to the lab assistants busy with their work. Kramer followed her gaze.

"Ricardo, Heather, can you come over for a minute?" Kramer called.

Kramer introduced Ricardo Caney and Heather Dungan to Sammie. "This lady here," he pointed at her, "wants to understand what we're doing in the lab, besides helping women get pregnant. She doesn't know a thing about CRISPR. But, be careful, she's a reporter."

The young scientists, Kramer's star researchers, gestured for Sammie to follow them to a corner of the lab where several battered easy chairs surrounded a cluttered coffee table.

"So, what do you want to know?" began Ricardo, getting up and heading to the nearby whiteboard to erase the diagrams already scrawled there.

"Well, this CRISPR process. What is it? And why are you doing it?" Sammie settled into her chair and set up her gear again.

"Basically," said Heather, "we're trying to cure a genetic disease called Niemann-Pick that affects mostly Jews." She explained that Niemann-Pick usually kills babies in the first year or so of life, adding that that is what had happened to Kramer's baby son. He and his wife were carriers, but they didn't know it. "We're trying to find the bad gene and take it out of the embryo and insert a healthy version of the gene in its place."

"Wow," Sammie said. "That is really possible?"

"In theory, yup," said Ricardo, picking up a black dry-erase marker to begin his own diagram.

So, CRISPR, he explained, stands for "Clustered Regularly Interspaced Short Palindromic Repeats." Sammie was lost already but kept writing and taping. Observing her bewildered look, as if she was a specimen under a microscope, Ricardo started over, with just the basics. He reminded her what DNA was and how it works with a related molecule, RNA, to make protein. And that many proteins are enzymes that control reactions inside cells, adding, "All life is chemistry."

How reductionist, Sammie thought.

Ricardo plunged on, clearly in his element. He explained that enzymes are made up of amino acids all strung together in a long line. Genes are the blueprint for the amino acids. So if there's a mistake, such as a mutation in the gene itself, or if, in the process of making the enzymes, the amino acids get strung together incorrectly, the protein (the enzyme) is either missing or screwed up.

Sammie hazarded a guess, "And that's what happens with Niemann-Pick?"

"Bingo. With Niemann-Pick, an important enzyme is missing." The result, he added, is that the baby's cells can't chew up fats correctly, so the fats clog up tissues all over the body and the child ultimately dies.

Sammie could feel his excitement and her own. "So, you can really fix this with CRISPR?"

"That's the goal we're working toward," Ricardo said.

"How would you do it?" By now, Sammie was genuinely fascinated.

CRISPR, he explained, is sort of a chemical "hit man."

She arched an eyebrow. "A hit man?"

"Sort of." Ricardo grinned. The idea, he explained, was to concoct the "hit man," a special molecule, a kind of chemical robot called "guide RNA." When this hit man is injected into a cell, it cruises along the strand of DNA like that little pull thing on a zipper, looking for the exact spot on the DNA it has been programmed to find. In this case, he added, the "hit man" would stop at the Niemann-Pick gene.

"Okay," Sammie said, envisioning a little robot sliding along a zipper.

The little robot, Ricardo went on, carries a tiny backpack, a protein that acts like scissors. The scissors part is called Cas9.

When the scissors hit the right spot, it breaks the DNA, ripping the two strands of DNA apart.

"Ouch!" Sammie said.

"I know. The cell really does say 'ouch,'" Ricardo said.

What happens next, Ricardo continued, is that the cell tries to repair its broken DNA. For a while, it succeeds. But the CRISPR robot keeps attacking again and again in the same spot, forcing the cell to keep trying to repair itself. Eventually, the cell can't keep up and makes a mistake.

"Sounds bad," Sammie said.

"It is," agreed Ricardo. The result is that the DNA gets messed up and boom, the cell ends up with a bad gene and a damaged or missing enzyme.

"But can't you make a new CRISPR or something to put in a good gene to replace the bad one?" Sammie was getting it.

"Yup, though nobody's done that yet with Niemann-Pick."

"But that's what you're doing?"

"You got it."

Sammie wasn't so sure of that, but she thanked him and Heather, said goodbye to Kramer, and headed to her car.

6

THREE YEARS EARLIER, SUMMER 2015

K ramer's lab was humming, as usual.
Most of the thirty-odd fellows, research associates, and postdocs were in the main section working in the arena that had made Kramer's lab world famous—the genetics of kidney disease.

To be honest, the kidney research bored Kramer to tears. He increasingly found himself taking breaks for computer solitaire instead of reading the team's latest results on kidney genetics. But it was a perpetual gold mine. In vitro fertilization was a huge moneymaker, too, and it bothered Kramer not at all that the lab was raking in money on the backs of frantic couples desperate to get pregnant.

The newbies in the lab were content just to get their names on the steady stream of kidney and IVF papers in first-tier journals, with Kramer as lead author, of course.

But now, CRISPR. That's where the real glory lay, and everybody in the lab knew it, especially Kramer's favorites, Ricardo and Heather. Kramer had long felt that there was something special in these two that the others lacked. Ricardo was tall and lanky, a former college swimmer, whose relaxed body language hid a tenacious mind. He had recently married his high school sweetheart and was thrilled that their first baby was on the way. He would clearly be a tender father, but there was no hiding his fierce competitive streak.

Heather, who was only slightly behind Ricardo on the postdoc treadmill, was pretty, slight, single and a Phi Beta Kappa grad from Williams. Her basic lab rat uniform consisted of a purple tunic over tight black jeans. She had long since ditched her last pair of heels.

Ricardo's and Heather's workstations had recently been moved to a closed-off space reserved for them alone. The other researchers had buzzed about that for a few days, then had collectively shrugged and gone back to their own work.

It hadn't taken much for Kramer to lure Ricardo and Heather away from kidney research. He explained their new project—the genetics of Niemann-Pick, a disease so rare they'd actually Googled it surreptitiously as he was speaking. Kramer had also not-so-subtly suggested that there could be a Nobel in this if they showed CRISPR could cure Niemann-Pick.

Raising their salaries had helped clinch the deal, as had beefing up their titles. The fact that Kramer had insisted their work be secret, lest word get out to competing scientists, had only added to the intrigue. The only dicey moment had come when Heather had ingenuously asked why they should bother studying Niemann-Pick if it was so rare.

Kramer had actually flinched, collapsing hard against the back of his chair as if from a body blow. Heather froze. Ricardo dove forward as if to catch Kramer. For a long moment, nobody said a word.

"Isaiah," Kramer had finally said.

Heather and Ricardo stared at him, then at each other.

"Isaiah?" ventured Heather.

"My son. My baby son. Niemann-Pick is like Tay-Sachs, a disease that can be carried by Ashkenazi Jews." He told them that Isaiah had been his fourth child and that his other three had not had the disease, though they were carriers. Isaiah had died just after his first birthday.

"Oh, my God," Heather whispered. "I am so sorry. I am so sorry."

"I am, too, Dr. Kramer," Ricardo added.

Kramer forced himself upright. He tightened his shoulders, placed his forearms firmly on his desk, and looked them in the eyes.

"Just cure this sucker. That's all I ask. And the sooner the better."

The meeting obviously over, Ricardo and Heather had nodded and hurried out, heading straight to their lab area. They had wasted no time, attacking their computers, reading bits of information aloud to each other, printing out relevant research papers, and scribbling in their lab notebooks.

The Niemann-Pick gene, they had quickly realized, was a big one, on the short arm of chromosome 11. Their ultimate job would be to pluck that deadly gene out of the DNA in a fertilized egg from a couple at risk for Niemann-Pick and insert in its place a healthy version of the gene instead. They were both instantly intrigued.

It soon became apparent that infants born with this horrible disease went through utter misery in their short lives. As an expectant dad, Ricardo couldn't help but worry about all the biological hurdles every fertilized egg and embryo has to pass through. And embryos with recessive but potentially deadly genetic defects? He could barely imagine being a parent in that situation.

In a government database called NCBI, the National Center for Biotechnology Information, they found mountains of genetic information on inherited disease, all written in the familiar DNA code—the four "letters," A, C, T, and G. With a click of the mouse, they could access scientific papers with dozens of coauthors each. There were thirty-nine recent papers, they quickly found, for one type of Niemann-Pick alone.

"What are we looking for, exactly?" asked Heather.

"This. I got it," said Ricardo. He pointed on his screen to a long string of A's, C's, T's, and G's. "It's the whole coding region of the Niemann-Pick gene."

Heather got up and leaned forward to see Ricardo's computer. There it was:

Nucleotide Sequence (1896 nt):
ATGCCCGCTACGGAGCGTCACTCCGCCAGAGC
TGCCCCAGGTCCGGCCGGGAGCAGGGACAAGAC
GGGACCGCCGGAGCCCCCGGACTCCTTTGGATG
GGCCTGGTGCTGGCGCTGGCGCTGGCGCTGGC
GCTGGCGCTGGCTCTGTCTGACTCTCGGGTTCT
CTGGGCTCCGGCAGAGGCTCACCCTCTTTCTCC
CCAAGGCCATCCTGCCAGGTTACATCGCATAGT

GCCCCGGCTCCGAGATGTCTTTGGGTGGGGGAA
CCTCACCTGCCCAATCTGCAAAGGTCTATTCACC
GCCATCAACCTCGGGCTGAAGAAGGAACCCAATG
TGGCTCGCGTGGGCTCCGTGGCCATCAAGCTGT
GCAATCTGCTGAAGATAGCACCACCTGCCGTGT
GCCAATCCATTGTCCACCTCTTTGAGGATGACAT
GGTGGAGGTGTGGAGACGCTCAGTGCTGAGCCC
ATCTGAGGCCTGTGGCCTGCTCCTGGGCTCCAC
CTGTGGGCACTGGGACATTTTCTCATCTTGGAA
CATCTCTTTGCCTACTGTGCCGAAGCCGCCCCC
CAAACCCCCTAGCCCCCAGCCCCAGGTGCCCC
TGTCAGCCGCATCCTCTTCCTCACTGACCTGCA
CTGGGATCATGACTACCTGGAGGGCACGGACCC
TGACTGTGCAGACCCACTGTGCTGCCGCCGGGG
TTCTGGCCTGCCGCCCGCATCCCGGCCAGGTGC
CGGATACTGGGGCGAATACAGCAAGTGTGACCT
GCCCCTGAGGACCCTGGAGAGCCTGTTGAGTGG
GCTGGGCCCAGCCGGCCCTTTTGATATGGTGTA
CTGGACAGGAGACATCCCCGCACATGATGTCTG
GCACCAGACTCGTCAGGACCAACTGCGGGCCCT
GACCACCGTCACAGCACTTGTGAGGAAGTTCCT
GGGGCCAGTGCCAGTGTACCCTGCTGTGGGTAA
CCATGAAAGCACACCTGTCAATAGCTTCCCTCCC
CCCTTCATTGAGGGCAACCACTCCTCCCGCTGG
CTCTATGAAGCGATGGCCAAGGCTTGGGAGCCC
TGGCTGCCTGCCGAAGCCCTGCGCACCCTCAGA
ATTGGGGGGTTCTATGCTCTTTCCCCATACCCC
GGTCTCCGCCTCATCTCTCTCAATATGAATTTTT
GTTCCCGTGAGAACTTCTGGCTCTTGATCAACT
CCACGGATCCCGCAGGACAGCTCCAGTGGCTGG
TGGGGGAGCTTCAGGCTGCTGAGGATCGAGGAG

ACAAAGTGCATATAATTGGCCACATTCCCCCAGG
GCACTGTCTGAAGAGCTGGAGCTGGAATTATTA
CCGAATTGTAGCCAGGTATGAGAACACCCTGGC
TGCTCAGTTCTTTGGCCACACTCATGTGGATGA
ATTTGAGGTCTTCTATGATGAAGAGACTCTGAGC
CGGCCGCTGGCTGTAGCCTTCCTGGCACCCAGT
GCAACTACCTACATCGGCCTTAATCCTGGTTACC
GTGTGTACCAAATAGATGGAAACTACTCCGGGAG
CTCTCACGTGGTCCTGGACCATGAGACCTACAT
CCTGAATCTGACCCAGGCAAACATACCGGGAGC
CATACCGCACTGGCAGCTTCTCTACAGGGCTCG
AGAAACCTATGGGCTGCCCAACACACTGCCTACC
GCCTGGCACAACCTGGTATATCGCATGCGGGGC
GACATGCAACTTTTCCAGACCTTCTGGTTTCTCT
ACCATAAGGGCCACCCACCCTCGGAGCCCTGTG
GCACGCCCTGCCGTCTGGCTACTCTTTGTGCCC
AGCTCTCTGCCCGTGCTGACAGCCCTGCTCTGT
GCCGCCACCTGATGCCAGATGGGAGCCTCCCAG
AGGCCCAGAGCCTGTGGCCAAGGCCACTGTTTT
GCTAG

"Good Lord," said Heather. That's a huge gene."

Their task now was to find a specific sequence amid all those A's, T's, C's, and G's to be the spot that they would aim their guide RNA, that CRISPR robot. Once they got the right target, it would be like ordering the robot to go to a certain house on a certain street and kill a specific person in that house.

All they had to do was type in the sequence they were interested in and order their custom-made CRISPR kit online. Just specify what they wanted and it would arrive. Like ordering men's boots, black, size 12 from L.L.Bean. The only difference was the boots would arrive by snail mail and their order, by email.

As Ricardo typed, Heather watched his screen. She was still amazed that there were CRISPR stores like the one they used, GeneShop, out there in cyberspace. And that anybody, anywhere could just go online and order a CRISPR kit. In fact, so-called biohackers did it all the time. In garages and kitchens all over the country, people were buying CRISPR kits and injecting themselves. The idea, according to the biohacker mentality, being to enhance various bodily functions and to sidestep the slow march of mainstream science.

"Insane." Heather shook her head. Ricardo agreed. But for legitimate scientists, being able to order $150 CRISPR kits online was a godsend, a way to avoid hours of tedious lab time.

Ricardo clicked the BUY button, raising his hand with a flourish. "Done. Now we just sit back and wait."

A FEW DAYS later, Heather logged on and quickly found a message from GeneShop. She reached over to tap Ricardo on the arm. He quickly put down his coffee and fired up his own computer.

There it was. A CRISPR kit, all ready to go. He strolled over to Kramer's office, caught his eye, and jerked his head in a come-with-me signal. Kramer nodded, waited a minute, then followed Ricardo to the men's room.

After making sure they were alone, Ricardo grinned and, keeping his voice low, told him the guide RNA had come in. Kramer's eyes lit up as he told Ricardo to print it out for him later, specifying to do that only when no one else was near the printer.

Toward the end of the day, when most of the lab had emptied out, Ricardo stood by the printer and nodded to Heather to send the sequence. Ricardo snatched the paper as soon as it rolled out and strolled over to Kramer's office.

"Here it is," Ricardo said moments later, excitedly handing his boss the printout that could change everything. Ricardo hovered as nonchalantly as he could in the doorway as Kramer took the paper, returned to his desk, and scrutinized the sequence.

Kramer read the letters off silently to himself:

GGTGCCAGACATCATGTGCGGGG

The guide RNA was aimed at the healthy version of the Niemann-Pick gene. Kramer's thoughts raced: He had told Ricardo and Heather that their mission was to find the lethal version of the Niemann-Pick gene in an embryo and replace it with the healthy form of the gene, to cure the disease. And that was true. He did want, eventually, to cure Niemann-Pick. But it wasn't the only truth. Kramer smiled to himself. First, his covert goal was to do just the opposite, take out a healthy gene and replace it with a bad one.

"Go for it," he spoke loudly so Ricardo, still in the doorway, could hear. "Keep me posted."

Ricardo walked quickly back to Heather, then together they went to the storage area of the lab. They took out a sample of normal human cells they had ordered from a commercial DNA site. They also took out cells they had obtained from a baby who had died of Niemann-Pick, cells they had gotten from a Niemann-Pick research and support group.

Whispering step-by-step directions to herself, Heather gloved up and retrieved two sterile syringes from the supply cabinet. She then injected the CRISPR material—the guide

RNA—into both types of cell, the healthy ones and the ones from the baby with Niemann-Pick.

With growing excitement, Ricardo and Heather watched to see if the DNA had been cut in either cell. They looked up at each other, eyebrows raised practically to their hairlines, mouths agape. CRISPR had performed perfectly. Like the little molecular robot it was, the guide RNA had scanned the DNA and landed on the healthy version of Niemann-Pick gene in the test tube with the healthy cells.

In the other test tube, the one with the deadly, mutated Niemann-Pick gene, nothing happened, just as expected. Since the DNA in the unhealthy cell had a different sequence of letters, there was no matching DNA sequence for the guide RNA to find. This time, the "hit man" came up empty. Perfect. The "hit man" had found only the small stretch of DNA that it was supposed to.

Heather and Ricardo indulged in a boisterous, albeit silent, high five. If they could cure Niemann-Pick, that could be the beginning of many other genetic cures they, and others, might achieve. They packed up the equipment for the night, tidied up their workspaces, and walked out together past Kramer's office, where the lights were still on.

He had been waiting for them and looked up as they neared his door. He raised his eyebrows hopefully. Wordlessly, they each gave him a thumbs-up.

7

SUMMER 2018

After Sammie left, Ricardo, Heather, and the other researchers closed up shop and, one by one, gathered their things and went out to their cars. Suddenly alone in the now-silent lab, Kramer tilted his chair back and sagged into it. "Fuck," he said to himself. His head drooped down toward his chest. He hoisted his feet up onto the lab counter.

All those plaques on his wall? *Worth shit*, he thought. The six-bedroom house in Brookline? A fucking trophy. Ellen? Did she really love him? Did his kids? Did they even really know him? Nobody did.

Letting his eyelids close, he drifted, not into sleep, but into the deep well of sorrow and rage that had occupied a corner of his heart for as long as he could remember.

After destroying Lisbett Seidl's first batch of eggs those long years ago, Kramer had felt that urge, that rage, again with other IVF patients. He had had one couple—the husband's name was Gunther—whose name had also jogged his memory from his teenage reading. Gunther, as in Hans Gunther, who had been Seidl's boss at Theresienstadt.

As before, Kramer had waited until the couple went through several rounds of IVF and had finally produced healthy eggs and healthy sperm. He had personally fertilized the eggs. Then, alone at night in the lab, he had looked under the microscope, proud of these potential human beings. His creations. A feeling almost like fatherly pride swept through him, but that feeling was abruptly interrupted by an even more familiar feeling: rage. He dutifully counted the chromosomes, then paused for a moment and reached for the alcohol, which he poured over the just-fertilized eggs. Done. No baby for this couple. Not this time.

He had done it another time, too, with a couple whose last name was Rahm. Again his memory had clicked in. A First Lieutenant Karl Rahm had been commandant of Theresienstadt until the SS abandoned the camp in May 1945. Another night alone in the lab. Another fleeting feeling of pride at having helped a desperate couple create fertilized eggs. Then, another dousing of the eggs with alcohol. As it turned out, this had been the couple's last chance at conceiving. They kept trying IVF for six months more, but had been unable to produce any viable eggs.

Usually, he knew, he could temporarily forget these feelings of rage and sorrow when he was with his patients, or when
an experiment was going exceptionally well, or when one of his
kids did something that triggered genuine pride in him, or once
in a while, when he was making love to Ellen.

But mostly, he had to admit, those feelings stayed with him
all the time, just below the surface.

No one except him knew that rage. Well, maybe that wasn't
quite true. He suspected that his mother, Jan, a sad but tough
eighty-five-year-old widow who lived alone in a well-appointed
condo several blocks from his house, knew what was in his
heart. His father, Joseph, had died several years ago from
Parkinson's. Jan had nursed him through that long illness with
the same stoicism that had gotten her through so much before
that.

Saul knew her story by heart. His mother had told it to him
often. Jan Schwartz Kramer was born in Vienna in 1933. Her
parents, Brigitta, a botanist and research scientist ahead of her
time, and Johann Schwartz, a physician, had two daughters:
Jan and her younger sister, Rachel. They lived in a small apartment, filling the space with books, a piano, and the Jewish
friends who comprised their world in the mid-1930s.

The Schwartzes and their circle were skeptical of the growing enthusiasm in Austria and Germany to unite the two coun-
tries under Nazism. By January of 1938, Brigitta and Johann
had begun discussing their terrible decision with Brigitta's
mother, Sarah. The Anschluss was now inevitable. The Nazis
were coming. The Schwartzes had to leave Austria, and fast.
They acquired the necessary papers for themselves, but
couldn't get them for Sarah. They knew that if they left Sarah

behind in Vienna, she would be alone, utterly unprotected, almost certain to die at the hands of the Nazis.

But it became a matter of desperate math. If all five of them stayed in Vienna, they would all die. If the young family left, without Sarah, they might live.

In February, a month before the Anschluss, Brigitta and Johann bundled up Jan, age five, and baby Rachel, age two, and stuffed clothes and as much food and water as they could carry into their rucksacks. Sarah accompanied them to the Wien Hauptbahnhof, the main train station in Vienna, to watch them board the train east to Paris, to leave their home forever, never to see her again. Jan would carry that image of her grandmother, alone in the train station, for the rest of her life.

"What happened to your grandmother?" Saul had asked when he was a boy.

"It's very, very sad," Jan had said, holding Saul close. "We had to leave her behind. The Nazis were coming. If we had stayed behind, they would have killed us all. We had to leave. And we had to leave my grandmother behind."

Saul had solemnly taken the story in. His mother's face told him everything. Her eyes were dry—her tears had been used up decades ago—but her mouth would go down at the corners, and her cheeks would sag. She would sigh and look off into space, seeing something that Saul could not see.

"What happened to Sarah?" Saul persisted, even though he knew.

"She just stood there, crying, waving a white handkerchief. We leaned out the window of the train as long as we could to see her until the train turned a corner."

Jan's family was sponsored by a family in Ohio after a long wait. And that is where they settled. But Sarah perished at Theresienstadt

"Why did the Nazis do that?" he'd asked.

"They hated the Jews."

Saul looked at his mother.

"Do you hate the Nazis, Mom?"

"They were very, very bad people," Jan would say.

Saul hated them. He never told his mother during these talks that he had nightmares every night after they talked about the Nazis.

Kramer slowly emerged from the familiar reverie and looked at the clock, 7 p.m. Ellen would be expecting him. She was not beautiful, his wife of so many years, but she was faithful. Not fascinating, but a good mother and a decent cook. It hadn't exactly been an arranged marriage, but when he had first introduced Ellen to his mother, his mother had strongly approved. That was all he needed. He had proposed almost immediately, more eager to please his mother than Ellen or even himself.

He shut down his computer. Draping his white coat over his lab chair, he turned off the lights in the lab and closed the door, defeat and despair replacing the confidence and conviction on display just hours earlier. Stopping to get his sports jacket from his office, he grabbed his briefcase and headed for his car.

8

SEPTEMBER 2018

It was the first day of school.

Sammie had gotten up at 6 a.m. to pack the kids' lunches and drive them to their separate schools. They each had cell phones, duly set up with parental controls, so that they could contact her or she them, in case of an emergency. The carpools for the ride home were all set. Maddy had promised to babysit as soon as she got home from high school, ready to hold down the fort until Bob or Sammie got home at 6 p.m.

Sliding into her desk at nine o'clock, Sammie picked up the *Daily*. She had two Page One stories, which, miracle of miracles, the copy desk had managed not to screw up too badly.

"Whatcha got going for today?" Joe Green asked, sitting down too close in a nearby chair.

"Another Chelmsford selectmen's meeting, I guess," Sammie answered, moving her chair away. "That's about it."

"How would you like to cover a story at the statehouse instead?"

"Really? What happened to Frank? Did he quit?"

"No, but there's some kind of #MeToo rally going on outside the statehouse. The powers that be thought maybe they should have a woman covering that."

Duh, Sammie thought. "Sure," she said.

"We think you could do a really good job," Joe said, reaching to pat her knee.

"Joe, stop that! You can't touch me," she exploded.

Joe backed off, but then couldn't resist saying, "And if you do a good job, and you're really nice, we might let you cover the statehouse permanently." He emphasized the word "let" to irritate her more. Typical.

"Joseph Green," Sammie said firmly, gathering her purse and notebook and heading for the door. "I always do a good job. And I'm already nice." She watched him skulk away.

THE #MeToo RALLY had been exhilarating. Both the *Daily* and the *Boston Times* had run pictures of the hundreds of women with picket signs, collectively raising their voices for change. Sammie eagerly jotted down every thought that crossed her mind. The *Times* had even snapped a picture of her earnestly taking notes.

THAT NIGHT, WHILE sitting at dinner with Bob and the kids, Sammie was still juiced up. "It was amazing. All these women, standing up to these creepy men."

Bob reached across the table for her hand. "It's about time." The boys stopped chewing for a minute and looked seriously at Bob. They had changed in subtle ways since he'd moved in and married their mom. They seemed more grateful, relaxed, free to be kids. Catching the intimate moment with Bob and Sammie, they pushed their chairs back, mumbled their excuses, and left the adults alone.

Sammie pushed her plate out of the way and put her hand on top of Bob's warm one. She poured them each another glass of wine. A feeling of gratitude enveloped her entire being.

"I feel so lucky," she mused, looking into Bob's eyes. Sometimes, she still couldn't quite believe they were married. She clasped his hand at the table and smiled.

THEIR COURTSHIP HAD been fast, but not rushed. After a few dinners in Cambridge restaurants, they had found it increasingly difficult to break away from their passionate embraces to say goodnight. Sammie had been nervous, too, of course, as well as excited. She had spent many an hour on the phone with her women friends analyzing this budding romance. Finally, she had decided to take the plunge—she needed more than a warm hug at the end of the night.

On the night Sammie had picked as *the* time, she'd taken the kids for sleepovers at their friends' houses and had gotten ready in her new off-the-shoulder black dress and a pair of black heels. She anxiously looked at herself in the mirror, trying not to think about how long it had been since she had been with a man, when Bob rang the doorbell.

"I couldn't get reservations till eight-thirty," he'd said shyly as he came in. "I guess we'll have to twiddle our thumbs till it's time to go," he'd said, half nervously, half sarcastically. Sammie had wondered if he'd already realized tonight was the night.

Sammie had poured them each a glass of wine, put on some soothing jazz, and slid down beside Bob on the couch. Their bodies touched as they kicked off their shoes and put their feet on the coffee table, wineglasses untouched. Sammie leaned into Bob's chest, and his arm instinctively went around her. They just fit together. She raised her face to his. He bent his down to kiss her. His mouth was so warm. He pulled her closer and she willingly obliged.

"Sammie?" He pulled away from her for a moment. "I don't want to rush you, but . . ."

"Please, rush me," she had said. They never made it to the restaurant.

He'd been a fixture in her life from then on. Week by week, the pattern began to feel comfortable, predictable. The kids began to take Bob's presence for granted, no longer surprised when he opened the front door with his own key and walked in with his arms full of groceries for dinner. Not that they didn't have questions.

One night, in particular, little Beau had gotten right to the point.

"Is he going to be our daddy?" he'd asked. Liam, trying to be cool, hadn't asked the question himself, but stopped playing on his phone to listen to the answer. Bob's head had jerked up, too, as he stopped reading his book to listen to Sammie's answer.

"No, sweetie. Bob is Mommy's friend. Your daddy will always be your daddy. But if we all have fun together, Bob might be over here more nights."

To her surprise, Beau had suddenly relaxed. "Okay," he said. Then he'd turned to Bob and asked, "Can you read me a story?"

Bob had put his book down, trying futilely to hide a smile. "Sure thing, Beau. You pick the book and get nice and cozy, and I'll come into your room in a minute."

Liam, still pretending not to listen, had followed Beau into the bedroom and climbed into his own bed. For show, he opened his book, but it was clear he wasn't actually reading. Watching them, Sammie realized that her boys were showing her that they accepted Bob not only for her, but for themselves as well.

Sammie had listened to Bob's baritone quietly from the doorway and wondered how long had it been since she had heard a man's quiet voice at bedtime.

9

OCTOBER 2018

B oston's #MeToo march had led to other demonstrations that Sammie had asked to cover. The big one in Washington, DC, was everything she had expected and more. The weather was gorgeous, still sunny but not hot, with clear blue skies. A perfect, exhilarating, early-autumn day.

They were all here, a million women, probably more, chanting, singing, marching with arms linked on the Mall. That wonderful, surging female energy was contagious, deliriously raucous. Anger was palpable, too, strong and empowering. So was joy, and the feeling that justice, denied for so long, would be denied no more.

There were women in pearls and flats carrying briefcases. Women in military garb. Women in sweatshirts and leggings. Women pushing baby carriages or wearing babies in snugglies on their chests. Marital or parental status, gender preference, and cultural identity aside, they were unified today, fighting for their rights and for their voices to finally be heard.

Woman after woman spoke of her fury about sexual harassment and abuse. This was about power. And respect. About being victims no longer. Sammie couldn't understand why Joe Green didn't see that his come-ons and incessant attempts to touch her were a violation of her body and mind. *He was not a bad guy*, she thought. *Why couldn't he get it?*

As the march wound down toward the end of the afternoon, she found a quiet park bench. Footsore but happy, Sammie opened her laptop, placed it on her knees, and put earbuds in her ears for some soothing Mozart. She reread her notes and began to write.

She wrote fast—she always wrote fast—sentences flowing out of her, almost before her mind had a chance to process them. That wonderful feeling, the piece writing itself. In minutes, she had 1,500 words, the max allotted for the next day's paper. She hit the SEND button, then sat back on the bench and watched as the remaining women lingered, still talking, slowly gathering up their signs and posters.

"Call or text me when the edits are done," she texted Joe.

Fifteen minutes later, he texted back.

"We didn't change a word, kid. Nice work. You're on Page One."

She pumped her fist in a silent "Yes" and proudly called Bob with her news.

"So, it was great?" he asked.

"Sweetheart, it was fabulous! I feel so energized," Sammie gushed, but she detected a hint of hurt feelings on the other end.

"But I really miss you," she added. "I can't wait to get home."

"Same here. We'll pick you up at the airport," Bob replied. "Let's do something with all four of us. Then, after the kids are in bed . . ." His voice trailed off.

"I'll attack that gorgeous body of yours," Sammie finished the thought.

"And I'll return the favor," he smiled as they hung up.

ON MONDAY MORNING, Sammie was back at her desk at the *Daily*, early, as usual, and in a great mood. As she had expected, the *Daily* had placed her piece prominently on yesterday's front page, with huge, accompanying pictures by a pool photographer that beautifully exemplified her words.

To her surprise and delight, the *Boston Times* had also run her piece. The *Daily* must have put her story out on the Associated Press wire, and the *Times* had picked it up as a sidebar to its own story.

Maybe this was the opening she had been waiting for. She had called the *Times* editor, Jake Gordon, several times over the last few months, as her frustrations with the *Daily* piled up. She had never been put through to him personally, though, always being shunted off to Human Resources, which had the same message each time: "Sorry, no openings at the moment."

But now, Sammie had a bit more ammunition.

With more confidence than she usually had, she dialed Gordon's office and emailed him as well, finding the courage to append her résumé, adding that she hoped he had noticed her #MeToo story in the *Times*. Jake Gordon emailed back almost immediately: "Of course I saw it. Who do you think snagged it off the wires?"

Typing furiously, Sammie emailed back instantaneously. "Thanks so much. I know the *Times* doesn't have any openings at the moment, but could I come in for a quick chat?"

This time, there was no instant reply. Sammie sighed, her good mood ebbing away. She picked up her purse and her laptop and stopped by Joe's desk to tell him she was off, once again, to scour Chelmsford for stories.

That afternoon, as she was trying to pump energy into a story about the Chelmsford finance committee, she checked her email again. Spotting the new message, her good mood bounced back.

"Sure. Come in next week. Call my assistant. Cheers, Jake," Gordon had written.

"Jake?" Were they already on a first-name basis? She made the appointment, and suddenly, the Chelmsford finance committee seemed more tolerable.

THE FOLLOWING WEEK, Sammie called in to the *Daily*, telling the city desk that she was sick and unable to come to work. She felt bad for lying, but not bad enough to change anything. This was her opportunity. She put on the slightly scuffed black heels hiding in the back of her closet, donned her best blouse and skirt, and drove to the *Times*. The newsroom was enormous, especially compared to the *Daily*. There were rows and rows of desks, printers humming, phones ringing. Pure heaven.

Jake Gordon's assistant beckoned to her, offered her a coffee, and seemed happy to chat a bit while Sammie waited. As she sipped her coffee, listening to the sounds of news being captured all around her, Sammie sized up the young-looking editor. He was handsome, his dark beard showing only a few signs of gray. Forty, she guessed, in pretty good shape. A runner, probably. Not skinny, but close to it.

She watched Jake Gordon hang up and wave a come-on-in. He got up from his desk to shake her hand.

"So, you want to work for the *Times*?" Jake leaned up against the edge of his desk. Like most newspaper people, he got right to the point.

"Your #MeToo march story was great," he said, walking back to his chair and sitting down. "I see your stuff from the *Daily* every once in a while. Especially when you scoop us, like that series you did on how few black city government officials there are in the state. We should have had that. Anyway, why do you want a job here?"

"Good Lord," Sammie blurted. "Why wouldn't I? I've outgrown the *Daily*. I'm ready for a national paper."

"Well, here's the deal," Jake started, leaning forward on his desk. "You're good. Keep it up." He told her to send him her best stuff, not every week, but whenever she had something special. He added, looking her straight in the eye, that he couldn't hire her now. "But I know who you are. Call me if you get an offer from any other paper."

"Thanks so much, Mr. Gordon," Sammie smiled, rising from her chair, and extending her hand.

"It's Jake."

10

TWO YEARS EARLIER, FALL 2016

It was midnight. Kramer was increasingly obsessed with CRISPR. He still marveled to himself that a technique that had once smacked of science fiction was becoming reality in his lab day by day.

He had finally gone home for dinner with Ellen, dutifully, albeit restlessly, watched the news, and even made love to her when they shut the TV off. Then, when he was sure she was asleep, he had crept out of bed, dressed in the dark in a pair of old jeans and a Harvard sweatshirt, and driven back to the lab.

Manuel, the Spanish-speaking janitor, who had worked there for years, offered a curious "*Buenas noches,*" as Kramer used his security code to get in the front door.

"*Buenas noches,*" Kramer had echoed automatically as the janitor gave him a last quizzical look before returning to his vacuuming.

Lately, Kramer had been feeling younger and more energized than he had in years. True, he had developed weird tics and occasional neck spasms that jerked his head to the left. But nobody seemed to notice. In fact, colleagues had been asking him what the secret of his newfound vigor was. Had he taken up jogging? Become a vegan? Discovered meditation?

"The secret?" he would say, barely hiding a self-satisfied smile. "I love my work."

In his office now, he took the DNA samples from his patients and carried them to his workstation in the lab. As he had done hundreds of times over the years, he fed the data into his computer, then watched as the results popped up on his screen.

"This is for you, Isaiah," he whispered.

Using the clinic's own genealogy kit, which he deemed better than the commercial kits used by the popular companies 23andMe and Ancestry.com, he began running preliminary family tree tests on the women in Josie's and Ashlyn's IVF group. He always did genealogy tests before the final preimplantation screening and implantation of the fertilized eggs into the women's wombs.

There were four other women in this night's group, but it was Josie Reimann Northrup and Ashlyn Graf Wilson whom Kramer was most interested in. He was almost positive that both women had German ancestors, judging from their middle names. In fact, Josie and her husband had whispered to each other in German at one of their visits. Josie's maiden name in particular excited him. It was a name he knew.

For a few years after high school, Kramer had more or less forgotten about his teenage obsession with the Nazis. College, then medical school and the PhD from MIT, internship, marriage, fatherhood. More than enough to crowd Nazis out of his mind.

But in the last decade or so, ever since he had surprised himself by destroying Lisbett Seidl's fertilized eggs, his obsession had been growing steadily. Now it was churning along full force. He followed newspaper and Internet stories about Nazis avidly, including some he had stumbled upon about a wealthy German family called the Reimanns—Alfred Reimann, Sr. and his son, Alfred Reimann Jr. Kramer learned that the Reimanns' company, the JAB Holding Co., owned all sorts of familiar chains, including Krispy Kreme donuts, Panera Bread, and Pret a Manger. He had been particularly intrigued by a 1978 report he had found about the family. For years right after that report, people, including younger generations of Reimanns, thought they knew everything that the older Reimanns had done to support the Nazis. But after a while, the younger Reimanns began to wonder if that report was accurate, and whether they did indeed know the whole story of their relatives.

So in 2014, the younger Reimanns had asked a professor at the University of Munich to dig deeper. As Kramer sat in his lab now, in 2016, work on that report was still supposedly secret. But, as with many secrets, there were whispers, references to what the professor might be finding in documents, family letters, old checks, and obscure websites and in emails among German and American Jews determined to know the full truth. Some of those bits of information had reached Kramer's ears. Among the most tantalizing was that the Reimanns had been donating money to the paramilitary SS even before the Nazis came to power. In his mind, there was no question that the Reimanns had long-standing Nazi connections.

Tonight, as these thoughts ricocheted around his brain, he adjusted the lights, got out his materials, and set to work with his genealogy protocol.

"Bingo," he said softly to himself. Josie and Ashlyn both had Germans in their families going back for generations. None of the other women did. And because of her name, Josie Reimann Northrup could very well have been a direct descendent of Nazi sympathizers. Whether her friend Ashlyn's ancestors had actually been Nazis, he couldn't know. But the odds were good. It was enough. These two women were just what he was looking for.

He managed to get home by 4 a.m. and slide into bed without waking Ellen. He was snoring heavily when she began to stir at 7:30, rolling over into him.

She kissed his cheek, waking him. They didn't make love often, but when they did, it left Ellen feeling cheery, sometimes for several days.

"That was nice last night, honey," she cooed, not a suspicious bone in her body.

"It sure was," Kramer agreed. Better than Ellen would have ever guessed.

A WEEK OR so later, Ricardo and Heather waited excitedly to text Kramer until most of the other fellows had left for the day.

"R U free?" Ricardo typed.

The reply was instantaneous.

"Come on over," the doctor texted back.

Through the window in his office door, they watched as he waved them in and hung up his phone. He closed his laptop and leaned forward on his desk, anxious to hear what they had to report. Ricardo and Heather settled into their chairs.

"You guys look like the cat who swallowed the canary. Did you do it?"

"We did," answered Ricardo and Heather almost in unison.

"Careful," warned Kramer. "The walls have ears."

Ricardo glanced out into the hall. There was no one, but he lowered his voice anyway. He explained that he had been able to retrieve the Niemann-Pick gene, the whole thing, out of cells from babies who had died of the disease. It had been easy to get families to allow the world-famous Kramer lab to study their babies' cells.

Now, Ricardo explained, there was no Niemann-Pick gene anywhere left in those cells. They had also gotten healthy cells from babies who died from other causes. They were good to go.

"What did you do with the bad genes you took out of the Niemann-Pick babies?" asked Kramer, trying to keep the excitement out of his voice.

"In the fridge, all labeled, more than a dozen samples," answered Heather.

"So, should we go ahead and insert the healthy gene into the cells we took the bad genes out of?" Ricardo asked. He could practically see the scientific paper they would write. Not to mention the headline in the *New York Times*: "Scientists Use CRISPR to Cure Fatal Genetic Disease."

Kramer's voice interrupted his thoughts.

"Let's go."

The three walked over to Ricardo's and Heather's lab stations. Everybody else had long since left. Outside, the sun was setting, casting a lavender glow on low-lying clouds.

"You're sure this is the healthy gene?" asked Kramer as he filled his syringe with the CRISPR material. Ricardo and Heather nodded. Kramer emptied the syringe into the vial containing the defective cells.

Ricardo reminded Kramer that they had earlier attached some green fluorescent protein to the CRISPR concoction. It would light up bright green when they put it under ultraviolet light.

It didn't take long for CRISPR to insert the healthy gene onto chromosome 11, where the deadly, mutated form of Niemann-Pick had been.

"Holy shit," Kramer exclaimed. "There it is. Well done, guys." The gene glowed green.

The next step was to see if the gene was actually working, that is, making the right enzyme.

"It is! Look!" exulted Ricardo, staring through the microscope. The three stood there, half dumbfounded, half excited beyond belief, toasting each other with imaginary champagne glasses. It was the proof they had been hoping for, that it was possible to take out a bad gene and insert a healthy one. If this worked in embryos, they could save babies from getting Niemann-Pick.

"Proof of principle," Kramer murmured. The sweetest words a scientist could hear short of a Swedish voice on the phone saying, "This is the Nobel Prize committee and . . ."

KRAMER STAYED BEHIND after Ricardo and Heather left. He could feel his pulse thumping in his neck. He went to where he had stored the fertilized eggs from Josie's and Ashlyn's group. It had taken several cycles of IVF for the women to produce these precious eggs, but thanks to Kramer's skill, they had finally been successful.

Tonight was the preimplantation genetic screening, the so-called PGS tests, for all the women in the group who had managed to produce healthy eggs.

He consulted his notes, carefully matching them to the labels on the samples. He studied them carefully under the microscope. One woman's fertilized egg contained an abnormal number of chromosomes. No point in implanting it. The poor woman would not conceive in this cycle. He would have his nurse schedule a consult with her the next morning. Too bad, but this was only her first chance and the whole point of preimplantation screening was precisely this—to find and discard any potential embryo that was bound to fail.

He worked efficiently. The other fertilized eggs were all euploid, meaning each had exactly the right number of chromosomes. He double-checked Josie's and Ashlyn's fertilized eggs. They were healthy.

Finally, the moment of truth. He had waited for years for this moment, never quite sure it would really happen, and here it was. Finally, he would get some relief.

He filled a syringe with the CRISPR preparation he had made. Holding his breath, he slowly depressed the syringe into Josie's eggs. If all went as planned, CRISPR would remove the healthy gene. He would then insert the lethal Niemann-Pick form of the gene. With luck, the bad gene would land right where the healthy version had been, on the short arm of chromosome 11.

Next, he performed the second part of his plan. In addition to the lethal Niemann-Pick gene, he inserted what he thought of as his decoy gene, something that would throw pediatricians off the track when Josie inevitably began taking her baby to doctors.

The stealth gene was MSH2, a gene known to produce lots of mutations. When it's functioning right, the gene makes proteins that help damaged DNA repair itself. When it's mutated, it causes havoc, including a problem with a clumsy name: Constitutional mismatch repair deficiency syndrome.

The beauty of this, Kramer knew, was that this syndrome produces symptoms very similar to a disease that, like Niemann-Pick, appears in early childhood: neurofibromatosis type 1. Among other things, this disease is almost a slam dunk to diagnose. The child gets a number of flat, light brown spots on the skin, freckles in the armpit, pea-sized bumps under the skin. Scary symptoms for parents, but a doctor looking at an infant with these symptoms would never think of Niemann-Pick and could honestly assure parents that the problem was likely neurofibromatosis. And that as long as the symptoms remained mild, the child would probably go on to have a normal life span.

When the deed was done, Kramer allowed himself a huge sigh of relief. He would implant the doubly altered egg tomorrow in Josie's uterus. He decided to save Ashlyn's frozen eggs for a few months to see what would happen with Josie. Assuming Josie's pregnancy proceeded normally, her baby, her little German baby with its Reimann ancestors, would die by his or her first birthday.

Finally, sweating profusely, Kramer collapsed in a nearby chair. He stared at the petri dishes sitting on the lab counter.

Dr. Saul Kramer, once named as one of Boston's best doctors by *Boston* magazine, had expected to feel elation at this point. He had even expected to feel some guilt. After all, he knew that what he was doing was abhorrent. But all he could feel right now was the bittersweet taste of revenge.

11

NOVEMBER 2018

I t was the night of the town meeting, one of the few times of the year Sammie didn't really mind covering Chelmsford.

Town meetings usually dragged on for hours, which meant she wouldn't get home until midnight. It also meant she'd be exhausted tomorrow morning. But the meeting itself was so "New England," so down-home, so small-bore democracy that Sammie always felt a shiver of admiration for the good souls who cared enough about their community to turn out and debate the burning issues of the day.

Well, "burning" was not exactly accurate, she mused, driving back to the *Daily* after the meeting. She could have filed her story from home, but she felt she could concentrate better in the newsroom. "Boring as shit" would be a better description. Still, she would find a way to make her story sing. She always did.

Back at her desk, Sammie glanced around the nearly empty newsroom. The night editors were there, chugging coffee and gossiping to keep themselves awake. A couple of sportswriters were still there, winding up their stories on local high school games. Joe Green was there, too, tapping his fingers impatiently on his desk, waiting for her story.

"How long?" he called over to her as she stowed her purse and started to sit down. He beckoned her over.

"How long will the story be? Or how long till you get it?" she asked, approaching his desk.

"Both," he said grumpily. He was in a bad mood for some reason. Sammie thought his eyes looked funny. He had been known to drink on the job when he was on night duty.

"A thousand words, half an hour," she answered. She shrugged off his gloomy look. Sammie could never figure out his moods. Most of the time, she didn't even try. He'd been grouchier than ever lately, though. Maybe another romance gone bad.

She began typing. It was the usual town meeting stuff. A vote (yes) to establish a municipal emergency ambulance service. A vote (yes) to support an arts center in the town hall. A vote (a narrow yes, after much debate) to transfer money to fix the ninth hole in the golf course. *Good Lord*, she thought, *all politics really is local*. A resounding "no" vote on letting property owners with big lots keep cows, horses, sheep, and pigs on their land.

She sent the story to Joe, who glanced through it quickly and passed it on to the copy editors. She could feel him watching her as she gathered up her laptop and purse, slinging one over each shoulder. She headed for the elevator, consciously putting his weird mood out of her mind.

He followed, unsteadily.

Just as the elevator door closed, he crashed in.

"Joe! What are you doing?" Sammie asked, surprised. She pushed the button for the street level.

Joe lurched toward her, letting the door close, then jabbed his finger on the emergency STOP button while they were between floors. He hurled himself at her.

"Bitch," he snarled. "You can't brush me off this time." He grabbed her by the hair with one hand and yanked her head back, hard. With his other hand, he pushed her against the wall of the elevator. As she tried to scream, he thrust his face onto hers and forcibly stuck his tongue in her mouth.

She choked, then in a flash remembered the self-defense moves she had learned years ago to protect herself, right after Brad had died. With all the force she could muster, Sammie jerked her right knee up hard into his groin.

"Bastard! Get off me!" she yelled. That was the other thing Sammie remembered—scream, yell, make noise. "Help!" she screamed, as Joe sank to the floor in pain. Nobody heard, of course, but she quickly flicked off the STOP button and hit the street-level button again, hard.

Joe was cursing, doubled over on the floor of the elevator.

"I should kick you, you asshole," she shouted. She didn't, but ran out of the elevator the second the door opened, purse and laptop thumping on her back.

Safe in her car, but still shaking violently, Sammie started the engine and was racked with sobs as she backed the car out of the parking lot while looking around frantically to see if Joe had followed her. He hadn't.

THE NEXT MORNING, running on three hours' sleep, adrenaline, and a lot of coffee, Sammie got to the newsroom by 10 a.m. She scanned the room. No Joe. She didn't realize how tense she had been until her body relaxed in relief.

Without speaking to anyone, she stopped at the bathroom to put makeup on the bags under her eyes and fluff up her hair. Then she went straight to the big, fancy offices on the other side of the building. Waving with feigned confidence to the secretary guarding the publisher's door, she knocked.

George Peabody was an old-line Boston Brahmin with coiffed white hair, a trim physique from hours on the squash courts at the Harvard Club, and manicured nails. He looked up from his desk. He didn't know most of his reporters, but Sammie had stood out since the day she was hired.

"Samantha Fuller, to what do I owe this pleasant surprise?" Gallant, with the exquisite manners of his class, Peabody gestured to the chair opposite his desk. "Great stuff on the march, by the way. I saw some of it made the *Times*." The praise was genuine.

"But why are you here?"

"Last night, here, at the office, Joe Green sexually assaulted me."

Peabody, clearly startled and concerned, got up and, signaling to his secretary to hold his calls, came around his desk to sit in the armchair closer to Sammie.

"What happened, Samantha?" he asked quietly.

"He trapped me in the elevator, yanked my head back, and stuck his tongue in my mouth." Tears sprang to her eyes. Sammie brushed them away harshly, wanting to be as strong as all those women she'd just written about. "I was petrified. I thought he was going to rape me."

"Did he?" asked Peabody gently.

"No. I mean, he's always putting his hands on me in the newsroom. I tell him not to, but he does it anyway." It wasn't rape, but she had thought it would be. "I can't work with him. I'll have to quit."

George Peabody looked her straight in the eye. Was that a tear she saw there?

"I won't let you quit, not because of this," Peabody said. He paused, took a deep breath, and asked, "Can I tell you something, off the record?"

This was not what she was expecting. "Okay," she replied, bewildered.

His daughter, he began slowly, was a lawyer, about Sammie's age. She was raped at work last year, when she was working late one night. It was a senior partner in her law firm. She quit. "It took her several months to tell me and her mother about it," he said ruefully. "She's been in therapy ever since and still hasn't gone back to work. We're suing the partner and the law firm."

"Oh, my God. I'm so sorry," Sammie said. "That's awful."

"So is what Joe did to you." Peabody picked up the phone and dialed the city room. "Is Joe Green there?"

Whoever answered said Green had called in sick, sounding terrible.

"Tell Green I need to speak to him today," Peabody said, hanging up and turning back to Sammie. In fairness, he told Sammie, he needed to hear Joe's side of the story. "But frankly, I believe you. We may have to call the police."

"The police?" Sammie stammered. The tears started again with a vengeance.

"It's an assault," said Peabody reasonably. "That's a crime."

"But my kids," Sammie's tears flowed copiously down her face. Her personal story would be plastered all over. Her career would be ruined. No matter how good a journalist she was, she'd always be known as the one who got attacked. She'd be victimized all over again. Sammie dabbed fruitlessly at the torrent of tears. She had thought that coming to Peabody was the right thing to do, but the possible repercussions of going to the police felt like it required more courage than she could muster.

He softened. "I understand. Let me talk to Green."

"Thank you. And no police?" she asked.

"I'll have to think about that. I don't want to cover up a crime. But I have something that may help you feel a bit better."

"I can't imagine what," Sammie murmured.

"We were going to announce this in a few weeks, but I think I can jump the gun," he said with a smile. "After all, I own the place."

"What?"

"How would you like to cover the statehouse, along with Frank?" Frank, the statehouse bureau chief, had been asking to have Sammie as second-in-command. There were always dozens of stories he couldn't get to by himself.

"Seriously?" Her jaw dropped and her eyes widened.

"Seriously. This is not charity, Samantha. You've earned it."

PEABODY DID NOT fire Joe Green right away. Green was no dummy. He had shown up with a lawyer for his meeting with Peabody. After all, it was just her word against his.

He denied everything. And he had more seniority at the paper than Sammie did. He was an editor; she was just a reporter.

Peabody had been unmoved by Joe's version of events, but cautious. It was clearly a case of "he said, she said." No witnesses. He had even harbored a soft spot in his heart for Joe Green. Until now. So he put Green on paid administrative leave.

A few weeks later, Sammie got a call from Peabody.

"Joe finally admitted everything." Peabody sounded weary but pleased. Joe Green was now under a restraining order not to come near Sammie or her family or to set foot back at the paper. He was fired. He had even said he wanted to talk to Sammie in person to apologize. Peabody told him he would pass that message along. Joe had also said he knew he should go into therapy. Peabody had strongly agreed.

"Wow," Sammie said. "How in heaven's name did you make this happen?"

"I didn't exactly make it happen, but I helped," Peabody replied. He explained that when he'd first confronted him, Joe had been angry and defensive. But he had grudgingly admitted to an alcohol problem and even admitted that he sometimes drank on the job. Peabody had informed him that that alone was grounds for dismissal and told him in no uncertain terms to go to Alcoholics Anonymous every day for at least two weeks without fail and then come back to talk again. Joe had actually managed to do that. He was not yet really in recovery—he had had several relapses—but he had at least taken in the idea of making amends and apologizing. Or so it seemed.

"Do you really believe that he wants to apologize?" Sammie didn't. Nor was she sure she would accept an apology from him.

"I'm willing to give him a shot," Peabody replied. Then he grinned. "You start at the statehouse on Monday. But there's one story I would like you to write first."

12

The story in the *Lowell Daily* was headlined "A #MeToo Moment in the *Daily* Newsroom." It ran on the front page that Sunday. Byline: Samantha Fuller.

This is a story I never thought I would write. As readers know by now, I have been covering the #MeToo movement for many months. I have interviewed dozens of women. I have admired their courage. I have believed their stories. I have been outraged by what they endured.

But never in all these months did I think I'd be writing about myself.

A few weeks ago, when I was working late on a story, the Daily *night editor, Joe Green, assaulted me in the elevator as I was going* home. I think he had been drinking on the job. We had had a friendly but somewhat awkward relationship. He had often touched me against my will, though not sexually. He also kept calling me "darling" even though I asked him not to.

That night, he barged into the elevator as I was on my way down. He pushed me hard up against the wall and forced his tongue down my throat. I was terrified. I fought back. I kneed him in the groin. He fell and I ran out of the elevator. The Daily fired him soon thereafter.

Recently, Joe conveyed to me through the Daily's publisher, George Peabody, that he wanted to apologize to me both privately and publicly, in a story in the Daily. He told Peabody that he has been living with his sister since he was fired. That he is going to AA and that he wanted to make amends.

I was very reluctant to do this. I was especially fearful that going public would harm my children, my husband, my parents, and myself. But I kept thinking of all the women who had summoned the courage to speak up. I ultimately felt it was almost dishonest of me to write about other women and hide my own story.

So last week, I met with Joe in Peabody's office with the publisher present. I asked Joe just to listen at first.

I told him how terrified I was when he attacked me. That I thought he was going to rape me, maybe even kill me. That he was much stronger than I was. That my heart was pounding. That I couldn't breathe. That I couldn't even scream because his tongue was in my throat. That my legs were shaking. That I peed in my pants. That I felt dizzy.

I told him that for weeks afterward I woke up every night with nightmares, screaming. That my kids would come rushing into my bedroom, terrified. They had already lost their father. They thought they were losing me, too.

I told him that I had begun seeing a therapist. That I still needed sleeping pills some nights. That I get panic attacks if I have to use an elevator.

As I spoke, I couldn't tell what Joe was thinking. He seemed to listen, but I wasn't sure. Finally, George Peabody asked Joe if he had anything to say.

At first, Joe didn't look me in the eye and kept staring at his shoes. But then he told me how angry he was at me for rejecting his advances, how enraged he was that his marriages and relationships had failed. That it was not fair. That he did not deserve to be treated this way by women. That he had his rights, too. At one point, he sprang to his feet, but Peabody was quick, and pushed him firmly back to his seat.

Peabody admonished him: "I thought you were here to publicly apologize, and to explain why you attacked Samantha so that the world might understand why some men abuse women. Why, Joe, why did you do it?"

Joe shrank into a smaller version of himself. He had no answers, no explanations because, simply, there are none. There are never any answers or explanations or reasons to do what he did to me.

"I'm sorry," he finally said grudgingly.

Maybe someday I will believe him.

13

DECEMBER 2018

One evening about a month later, Bob and Sammie were lying quietly on the couch, legs stretched out and cozily entangled on the coffee table, with sections of the *Daily* and the *Times* scattered around them. The kids were asleep, the dishes done, music playing softly.

Sammie was finally beginning to feel content again. The repercussions of going public with her story were not like anything she had anticipated. She had expected a torrent of support from women, which she got, and which buoyed her spirit tremendously. She had also been terrified that her boys would be harassed at school, that people would stare at her in the supermarket. And she had worried that her friends in the newsroom might consider her a traitor for "outing" the paper and that the male legislators at the statehouse, not generally an enlightened group, would sneer at her and maybe not talk to her for her stories.

Luckily, most of those fears had not materialized. Although her boys had taken things in stride, more or less, they had been teased by a few bullies taunting them about the idea of a guy sticking his tongue down their mother's throat. The boys told Sammie and Bob, who had gone together to see the school principal.

The principal, a gruff old Marine, had been wonderful. He called a whole-school assembly, at which Sammie had spoken, talking openly about sexual harassment and the abuse of women. Afterward, the principal had set up a secure system for kids who had been harassed to report those incidents. The system had been flooded with reports, mostly from girls, but from a few boys, too. The school had called in several psychologists and lawyers to address the complaints.

At the statehouse, Sammie had sensed a few sneers and muttered comments, but overall, the job was going well. The state legislature, she was dismayed to discover, was nearly as boring and dysfunctional as the Chelmsford selectmen, but in a far more extravagant setting. On the plus side, there were enough rumors of fundraising scandals, extramarital affairs, and tax cheating to chase down that Sammie was happy, even if most of what she dug up was not solid enough to publish. Still, it was big-time reporting, and she could feel, as journalists liked to say, the ink flowing in her blood.

The ringtone of her cell phone broke the quiet mood in the living room. Fumbling for the phone amid the newspapers, she found it under a pillow and saw Josie Northrup's name flash on the screen. Sammie's Mother's Day story about Josie late last spring had prompted a flood of calls and emails, mostly from women.

Some had reprimanded her for writing such a downer on Mother's Day. "Thanks for the nice gift," they wrote, sarcastically. Others, a number of them in tears, had thanked her profusely for reminding them how lucky they were to have living children, despite all the daily hassles and exhaustion of motherhood.

Josie and Sammie had stayed in touch after the story ran. In fact, Josie and Peter had invited Bob and Sammie over to dinner several times, and they had returned the favor. The Northrups were truly a lovely couple, and Sammie and Bob enjoyed spending time with them.

As the months ticked by, Josie seemed to be dealing with her grief. She had gone back to work part-time, seeing patients every morning, then taking afternoons off to see her own therapist and take long walks, often visiting Jamie's grave in Mount Auburn Cemetery.

Peter had managed to hold his own at the law firm, gratefully accepting smaller, less complicated cases until he felt ready to take on the big ones.

"Hi, Josie," Sammie began cheerfully, then stopped, heart pounding, when she heard Josie's sobs.

"Josie, what happened? What's the matter? Are you okay?"

Sammie waved frantically to get Bob's attention. He sat up straight, his brow furrowed, his hands reaching out to touch her. He put his arm around her as Sammie put her phone on speaker.

"It's, it's . . . ." Josie was practically screaming now, so loud Bob could have heard it without the speakerphone.

"It's Ashlyn. Her baby died suddenly tonight," Josie choked out the words. "I was with her, in the ER. We were holding Katy together."

Between sobs, she filled Sammie in. Until the very end, Katy had seemed sort of okay, except for a slightly enlarged spleen and difficulty swallowing. Ashlyn had kept trying to get a diagnosis. Katy had been in and out of the hospital a few times, tested for the most likely problems, been given IV fluids, and monitored. But as for a diagnosis, the doctors kept coming up empty-handed.

"Where are you now? Want me to come over?"

"Could you? We're back at Ashlyn's."

"I'm on my way."

Sammie raised her eyebrows in a silent question to Bob. He nodded. He would stay with the kids. Before Sammie ran out the door, she rushed to the kids' bedroom to give the boys an extra goodnight kiss. She needed the assurance that her own babies were alive and well.

SEVERAL DAYS LATER, Kramer was at his desk, sorting through journals, half-written articles his staff was working on, and piles of phone messages. He picked up the *Boston Times*.

"Holy God," he whispered. He put his coffee cup down so fast the coffee slopped out. His hands shook as he unfolded the newspaper. Finally. The news he had been waiting for. There, in the front of the obituary section, a picture of Ashlyn Wilson holding one-year-old Katy on her lap. The child's face was slightly distorted, just as Isaiah's had been. Though barely visible in the newspaper, there was a clear plastic feeding tube disappearing into the child's right nostril. The child's eyes puffy and closed. He read the obituary.

"Sixteen-month-old Katy Graf Wilson died last Saturday of unexplained causes. The child, daughter of Ashlyn Graf Wilson, a molecular biologist known for her research into malaria, died in the hospital after an unexplained illness.

"I wanted a baby so much," Ms. Wilson said in a short telephone interview with the Times. *"She was an IVF baby, and I was overjoyed to become pregnant and then, to become a mother." In the last few months, the grieving mother told the* Times, *she had taken Katy to doctor after doctor, but no one could diagnose her. It had been agony watching her decline. Toward the end, the child had had to have a feeding tube because she could not swallow. "She died in my arms."*

Services will be private. Ms. Wilson asked that in lieu of flowers, donations be sent in Katy's name to Save the Children.

Kramer studied the photo of Ashlyn and Katy, took a pair of scissors and clipped out the obit, placing it carefully in Ashlyn's folder in his safe, right next to the obit he had clipped earlier on little Jamie Reimann Northrup. In the stiff manila folders, the babies' obits rested next to the ecstatic, grateful letters and baby pictures both mothers had sent when their babies were born.

"Two down, one more to go," he murmured to himself, satisfied. He finished his coffee, mopped up the spill, packed his briefcase, and headed home.

LITTLE KATY'S MEMORIAL service was a haunting echo of Jamie's, only a few months earlier.

The IVF group had been there, of course, in full force. Like Jamie's service, this one was at the UU church in Cambridge. The young minister looked composed, as always, but this time, weary as well.

She wasn't used to babies dying. The last time, at the service for Jamie, she had managed to look Josie in the eye and telegraph her compassion. Now she had to do it all over again for Ashlyn. She was a minister. This was her job. The people sitting in front of her expected her, needed her, to make sense of this new tragedy. But how could she? None of this made sense.

AFTER KATY'S SERVICE, Josie and Peter, Ashlyn, most of the women from the IVF group, and Sammie adjourned to Josie's house. Both Josie and Ashlyn looked like hell. Josie was still as thin as the day Sammie had met her. Ashlyn had dark circles under her eyes; her cheeks were sunken, colorless. Neither had bothered with lipstick or mascara.

The women from the IVF group remembered Sammie. She had never gotten around to writing the story she had planned about IVF, having been swept away by her new statehouse duties.

And she had no story in mind tonight, either. She was here purely out of friendship for Josie, empathy for Ashlyn, and, she had to admit, curiosity about how these other women, so happy with their own healthy babies, would be able to console the grieving mothers.

She needn't have worried. The IVF women, grief-stricken and red-eyed, embraced Josie and Ashlyn with long hugs and more tears. They actually formed a circle, arms around each other's waists, a prayer circle by any other name. Eventually they sat, pulling their chairs up close to the coffee table that Josie had somehow managed to fill with wine and nibbles.

Eventually, sensing the group's love, Josie took Ashlyn's hand in hers and began to talk.

"I'm not just devastated," she offered tentatively, "I'm angry, too. Why? Why did this happen to Peter and me? Why did it happen to Ashlyn?" The whole thing made no sense, she went on. When he was born, Jamie was a healthy baby. Katy was, too. "Whenever I stop crying and start thinking, I go round and round in circles. I blame myself." Had she done something wrong? Had Ashlyn?

"You didn't do anything wrong, honey, and neither did Ashlyn," said one of the other women, handing her the box of tissues. The chorus of support was unmistakable.

"We watched you with Jamie," came one voice. "You were a terrific mother, too, Ashlyn," came another.

"I don't know," Ashlyn said. "Maybe I shouldn't have worked when she was little. I thought I could do it all, but . . ." she trailed off, her pain too great to continue.

"Then, what?" interrupted Josie. "If it's not our fault, then what happened?" Both mothers had taken their babies to doctor after doctor. Nobody could explain why they kept getting worse. Jamie's doctors said he had neurofibromatosis. But Katy didn't have that diagnosis. Yet they both died at close to the same age.

The group fell silent for a moment. Then Sammie took a deep breath, summoning her courage. "There's a thought I just can't get out of my mind."

"What?" asked Josie, staring straight at her.

"The IVF clinic," Sammie said. "You and Ashlyn used the same clinic, right?"

"Yeah," said Josie slowly, not wanting to follow this logic. "But, so did these women." She looked around the circle of sympathetic faces.

"You all got all the same drugs? All the same procedures?" Sammie persisted.

"More or less," said Josie. "We got individualized protocols, different hormone schedules and all that." But she had checked on the web. All the protocols were standard stuff, used by IVF clinics all the time.

THE QUESTIONING PETERED out, and Sammie didn't want to push it, especially with Ashlyn's loss so recent. Tonight, at least, there was nothing to do but shower Josie and Ashlyn with love and promises of moral support any time, day or night.

After Ashlyn and the others left, Sammie stayed behind to help Josie clean up. Peter, in sweatpants and a T-shirt, came out of his study to help. His eyes were puffy and red, the memories still too raw to bear.

"Something doesn't add up," Sammie said to them as they stood side by side loading the dishwasher. "Two babies from the same clinic, both dying so young? But with different symptoms. It's just weird."

The exhausted couple had no appetite for pursuing that thought. But Sammie could feel her reporter's instincts kicking in, especially as she remembered the subtle but clearly odd behavior Kramer had shown when she was with him. The answers were there somewhere. She knew it.

14

FEBRUARY 2019

Sammie was the last to leave the statehouse pressroom. As usual, the other reporters had left their desks strewn with books, press releases, and printouts of pending legislation, not to mention old coffee cups.

Sammie had filed her story on a proposed bill to regulate marijuana sales. She had also emailed the city desk at the *Daily* about a story for later in the week, another women's march. She wanted to make sure the paper would free up a photographer to meet her at the rally.

Then she texted Bob, who promptly wrote back that he was home, the kids were fine, and the water was already on a low boil for the pasta.

"Thanks, hon. I'll be there in fifteen," Sammie typed. "Love you."

She sat back. This whole business of Josie's and Katy's babies was eating at her. Two dead infants. Same IVF clinic. Different symptoms. No diagnosis for either. Sammie summoned her courage.

"Hi, Jake," she began her email to the *Boston Times* editor. "You said it was okay to call you 'Jake.' Anyway, can we talk? I may be on to a story that could be huge, and it belongs in the *Times*. I'd love to come in again to chat. Thanks, Samantha Fuller."

She didn't expect an immediate reply, and she didn't get one. After all, it was almost 6 p.m. and Jake Gordon was on deadline, too. At this hour, he would be in the last "budget" meeting of the day, where the final decisions were made about what stories would make Page One and which would be buried in the bowels of Metro. Sammie packed up her laptop and purse and headed to the elevator.

The next morning, she was delighted to see that an email from Jake Gordon had come into her inbox at 6 a.m. Jake Gordon was no slouch.

"Okay," he had written. "You got me. I'm curious. Make an appointment with my assistant for mid-afternoon later this week. Bring whatever you've got."

Yes! Sammie whispered under her breath, pumping her fist. *This could actually work.* She told Gordon she'd be there.

TWO DAYS LATER, Sammie once again sat across from Gordon's desk. The *Times* newsroom was in that lovely lull that happens just after lunch and before the deadline crunch.

"Whatcha got?" As usual, Gordon got right to the point.

"Well," Sammie began. "I can't prove anything yet. In fact, I only have two cases, plus a strong hunch. But here's the deal." She explained that she knew of two women who both went through IVF treatment at the same clinic outside Boston. They both got pregnant, finally, after a lot of ups and downs. They were ecstatic. Then, both their babies died around their first birthdays. Nobody could figure out why.

Jake Gordon sat up straighter and took his feet off his desk. He looked right at her.

"Go on."

"So, the weird thing is, these two women, Josie Northrup and Ashlyn Wilson—I'm not sure yet whether they'll let me use their names—are the only two women in their IVF group whose babies have died." There were half a dozen other women who all did IVF at the same time, she continued. They all got pregnant and all had their babies within a few months of each other. All those other babies were totally healthy. At least so far . . .

Sammie could see the wheels turning in Gordon's mind. This could be just coincidence. Nobody even knew what the babies died from, much less whether they died from the same thing. It didn't seem like it, judging from their symptoms, but something smelled off here.

"I know, I know, it could be coincidence," Sammie said. "But what if it's not?"

"If it's not, you have a helluva story. So, what do you need?" Jake asked.

"A job. Here. At the *Times*," Sammie grinned.

"Why not just write this for the *Daily*? A good story is a good story."

"C'mon, Jake. You know I've outgrown that paper. They've been good to me, well, except for one night editor." Sammie paused for a moment, recalling Joe's attack on her in the elevator.

"So how about this? You keep your suspicions to yourself for now. Keep doing your job for the *Daily* and poke around the story on the side."

In the meantime, he said, he would have a chat with the *Times* money people in the front offices. After all, the *Times* was doing well, all things considered. They had snagged a Pulitzer last year. The powers that be might be open to a new reporter.

"Of course, if they give me a slot, I'd have to put you on obits, at least for a while . . . ." he trailed off.

"I'll take it!" Sammie was no fool. Any job at the *Times* was a foot in the door.

"I actually like obits," she added, only half kidding. She loved writing about people's lives. She floated out of the newsroom, which was slowly coming to life like a bear emerging from hibernation—phones ringing, reporters grabbing stories off printers, the air electric.

"I love this," she smiled to herself, heading for the elevator and turning to look back over her shoulder at the organized chaos behind her. "God, I'd love to work here."

15

MARCH 2019

Kramer was frantic.

He hadn't slept well in weeks. He had deep, dark bags under his eyes. His face was gray. His hands shook so badly that he had taken to keeping them in his pockets. Just yesterday, he had yelled at Ellen when she accidentally broke a cup loading it into the dishwasher. She had looked at him as if he'd lost his mind as he stomped out of the kitchen.

In the lab, he was the proverbial bull in a china shop. He knocked over beakers, spilled reagents on the floor, bumped into other people, and radiated negative energy. He cursed at his computer and slammed his fist on the lab table repeatedly.

Nobody dared talk near him. His research fellows communicated among themselves by text and sign language.

The trigger for all the frenzy had come from China. A rogue Chinese scientist had sent shock waves around the world, announcing that he had used CRISPR to alter a gene in the embryos of twins—*human* twins.

The scientific world had gone crazy, horrified that the Chinese had violated the long-standing international agreement not to interfere with human embryos. Journalists were screaming about "designer babies." Nonscientists had no idea what the fuss was about, but sensed something evil in the word "CRISPR."

For Kramer, there were no such humanitarian thoughts. He was livid that the Chinese had scored another "first," regardless of the fact that everybody hated them for it. But more than pissed, Kramer was petrified.

Terrified that there would be an international crackdown on CRISPR research. Congress was already making noise about clamping down on gene editing research. Medical ethicists were huddling in committees, weighing the pros and cons of using CRISPR on fertilized eggs.

What if, Kramer fretted, IVF clinics were suddenly required to have two people in the room during all preimplantation screenings? That was the time that he needed to be alone.

It wasn't an idle concern. After all, there were similar rules already in place, such as the mandate that a nurse, or other personnel, be present when a doctor performs a gynecological exam on a woman. IVF procedures could be next. There was only one solution. He had to up his game. He had used CRISPR in almost a dozen fertilized eggs so far. He had to do more. A lot more. And fast.

"*Buenas noches*, Manuel," Ricardo said to the janitor, who smiled and nodded his acknowledgment of the greeting.

It was late, after 10 p.m. Normally, Ricardo did not go back to the lab in the evening, with his wife and baby at home, but he had forgotten his cell phone. He decided to make a quick trip back to the lab to grab it.

The door to the lab was closed, but it opened with a squeak when Ricardo pushed it. *Weird,* he thought. The lights were on in the far corner, where he saw a man hunched over a computer, his back to the door. Hearing the squeak, the man turned suddenly.

"Saul?" exclaimed Ricardo.

"What the fuck?" Kramer yelped. "What the hell are you doing here?"

"I forgot my cell phone," answered Ricardo, puzzled. "What are *you* doing here?"

"Working. What does it look like?" Kramer hastily logged off.

"I didn't know you were working at night," said Ricardo, trying to keep his tone mild. "You work so hard during the day. Don't you need a break?"

Kramer forced his shoulders down, leaned back in his chair and consciously arranged his face into a calm expression. He'd been taking a lot of Klonopin, the antianxiety drug, lately and wondered why it wasn't working. Tonight, he even added a Xanax to his regimen. He fought to keep his neck from spasming. He clasped his hands to hide their shaking.

"I like the peace and quiet," he said, unconvincingly. "Ellen has her book group tonight, so I thought I'd get a couple more hours of work done."

Ricardo let a few moments go by. Something didn't add up. The work he and Heather were doing on Niemann-Pick was going well. As far as he knew, Kramer had no complaints about their progress. Was he double-checking their work? Did he not trust them?

"Well," Ricardo shrugged, "don't stay too late. You need sleep like the rest of us mortals."

Kramer attempted a smile, but it was a rictus grin. His eyes were stony.

"See you in the morning."

On his way out to the car, Ricardo passed Manuel again.

"Manuel," he began. "Dr. Kramer, does he come here often at night?"

"*Si, si,*" nodded Manuel. "*Muchas noches.*"

LATE THE NEXT morning, as usual, the chatter among the fellows and post docs in Kramer's lab was minimal, their combined focus maximal.

Heather squatted down by the lab refrigerator, glancing over her shoulder at Ricardo, who was frowning over his laptop. As she did every morning, Heather dialed the combination that only she, Ricardo, and Kramer had. She began checking on the DNA samples, looking for the ones labeled as containing the deadly, mutated gene for Niemann-Pick. She had gotten the latest samples just a few days ago from families whose babies had died of Niemann-Pick.

She counted silently. Fifteen. Hadn't they just received twenty? She rooted around among the bottles but did not see anything else. Just fifteen. As she was about to close the refrigerator, her eyes locked on something else. Samples labeled MSH2. Weird. Another gene? What was it doing here?

Heather stood up, walked quietly over to Ricardo, and tapped him on the shoulder. He jumped slightly, so intent on his computer that he hadn't heard her approach. She put her finger to her lips and mouthed, "Shhhh."

"Lunch," she whispered. "Now."

He logged off, and, a few minutes later, they sat together at a distant table in the coffee shop.

"I was just in the lab fridge and there were only fifteen Niemann-Pick samples with the bad gene," Heather said. "We got twenty a couple of days ago. What happened to the other five? Do you know?"

Ricardo raised his eyebrows and stopped chewing the turkey and cheese sandwich his wife had packed for him that morning. Something wasn't right.

"Fifteen? I haven't touched any of them, and I assume you haven't, either."

"No, of course not. That only leaves one person who has access to that fridge."

"But he hasn't said anything about any other research," Ricardo was thinking aloud. "He used to tell us whenever he started some new protocol."

"He hasn't mentioned anything to me, either," mused Heather. "I have no idea where those samples could be." She paused, then added, "There's something else." She told Ricardo about spotting the vials of MSH2. "We're not working on that, are we?"

Ricardo shook his head, then ventured.

"Did I tell you that I came in last night and found Saul here in the lab, all by himself? I startled him. He was not exactly pleased to see me. I asked him why he was working so late, and he dodged the question."

"Weird. We're getting plenty done during regular working hours. . . ." Heather's voice trailed off, as she tried to imagine what else he could be working on that they didn't know about.

"You know what's even weirder?" Ricardo didn't wait for an answer. "You know that Manuel guy, the janitor? He was working last night. I asked him if Saul came here a lot at night. He said yes, all the time."

Back at their stations, Ricardo and Heather used Google Scholar to search for studies on MSH2. It made no sense. The main thing this gene seemed to do was increase the rate of mutations by messing up a cell's ability to fix mismatches in DNA.

"Shit," muttered Ricardo. "This could mess up genes all over the place. It could cause a whole slew of diseases. What the fuck is he doing with this?"

He printed out several scientific papers about the mutation-inducing gene and handed copies to Heather. She glanced at the titles. "Look. This thing can cause colon cancer and God knows what else. It has nothing to do with Niemann-Pick."

They quickly stuffed the MSH2 printouts in their backpacks to read more thoroughly at home and deleted the articles from their search history.

16

APRIL 2019

Josie and Peter were managing, but barely. They were both back at work, Josie just part-time, and work helped keep them somewhat sane.

But in the evenings, alone together in their apartment, they foraged for dinner, not having the energy or imagination to cook. They ate their cheese and crackers or yogurt or cereal in silence, watching but not taking in the nightly news. The outside world didn't matter these days. Only grief did.

Neither of them knew which one had closed the door to the small room that had been Jamie's, his crib still there, taunting them. But neither opened it. And neither had said a word about trying again, though they both suspected the other was thinking about it.

JOSIE HAD BECOME obsessed with obits. Ever since little Jamie's and Katy's deaths, she had taken to sitting at the kitchen table before work, flipping past the national news in the *Boston Times* and going straight to the Death Notices and obituaries. Mostly, the stories featured older people who had died after long lives. Sad, but not devastating.

Occasionally, there was a young person who died from a car accident or drowning or, increasingly, from gun violence. All too often, she saw pictures of once-vibrant women whose lives had been cut short by breast cancer.

She kind of knew her obsession with obits was a depressing exercise, but she didn't care. Her instincts told her something was off, that there was an answer out there, and she was the one who was going to find it. So she continued on grimly, morning after morning, searching for she didn't know what.

But what she saw this morning stopped her cold. An obituary about a baby, a fifteen-month-old boy named Henry David Steinberg. She froze, coffee cup in midair, then screamed.

"Peter, come out here! Hurry!"

Peter, towel tucked around his waist, came running out of the bathroom. "Are you okay?"

"Look at this." Josie shook the newspaper at him. Her face was white, her hands clenched. He grabbed the paper and sat down hard on the chair next to her.

"Oh, my God. Another one." He read the obit.

Henry David Steinberg, fifteen months old, died in the hospital on Friday of unknown causes. His parents, David and Suzanne

Steinberg of Waltham, were unable to be reached for comment, but Suzanne Steinberg's sister, Louise Beckman, said that the child had been conceived after a long battle with infertility. Mrs. Steinberg, her sister said, had used IVF (in vitro fertilization) to conceive, finally achieving a successful pregnancy after several cycles of treatment.

"My sister and brother-in-law are absolutely devastated," Ms. Beckman told the Times. *"They tried so long and so hard to have a baby."*

A memorial service has not yet been scheduled.

"This can't be a coincidence," Peter murmured. "Did this Steinberg couple go to Kramer's clinic? Was Mrs. Steinberg in your IVF group?"

"She was definitely not in our group," Josie said. "But she could have gone to Kramer's clinic."

"You have to find her." Peter's voice took on an urgency that was rare for him. "Track her down. Invite her over. This poor woman needs us, and we need her." Peter stood.

"Call Sammie, too," he said.

Retying his towel, he kissed Josie absentmindedly and walked as if in a trance back to the bathroom to finish shaving. Josie watched him, this dear husband who had been with her every horrible step of the way through IVF and was with her still through this unfathomable grief and these awful suspicions. The knowledge made her feel a little less alone in the desperate search to understand what had happened to their baby.

WHEN JOSIE CALLED, Sammie had just gotten to her desk and was checking the monotonous statehouse docket for what to cover.

"Hi, Josie." Sammie tossed the docket aside and leaned back in her chair.

"There's a third dead baby," Josie blurted, not bothering with pleasantries. "He was an IVF baby. He died on Friday. His obit is in the paper today."

Sammie sat silent, stunned. How could this be? She felt her hands go numb. Now she knew for sure that her reporter's instincts had been right all along, though, at that moment, it didn't give her the satisfaction she would normally feel. She reached for the *Times* and read the obit, as Josie listened on the other end.

"We have to contact that family," Sammie said. "I'll track them down and call you back."

She opened her laptop, checked out Suzanne Steinberg on Facebook, and found their phone number online. She left a message:

"Mr. and Mrs. Steinberg, you don't know me, and I hate to call at this tragic time. But I wanted you to know that I am a reporter and I have two friends who did IVF and had babies who died several months ago. I just wanted to reach out to you to offer my sympathy, and also to see if you would be up to talking. Your son is the third IVF baby I know of who has died at around one year old of mysterious causes." Sammie repeated her condolences, left her number, and hung up gently.

THE STEINBERGS DID not call back right away. But, a week later, they called Sammie. After several long and painful phone conversations, they agreed to meet with Sammie and Bob, Josie, Peter, and Ashlyn at Sammie's house.

That night, Bob put the boys to bed as Sammie arranged the crackers, cheese, grapes, and wine on the coffee table. She wasn't sure what snacks were appropriate under the circumstances, but went with the usual, thinking nothing was really appropriate for something like this. Bob joined the small, tense group as Sammie poured the wine and handed glasses around.

Formality gave way to shared grief. The women had long since given up makeup, their tears now the only marks on their faces. Mascara would just have made a mess anyway. David Steinberg looked like he hadn't shaved, or slept, in days.

After a short round of introductions, Sammie gently urged the grieving parents to recount their stories. After Josie and Ashlyn painfully recited their details in turn, everybody looked to Suzanne Steinberg.

Twisting a lapful of sodden tissues, she told of how thrilled she and David had been to finally conceive, and how devastated they had been when little Henry died. When she said that their baby, too, had been conceived at Kramer's clinic, the room went silent.

Suzanne dug into her capacious purse.

"I made copies for everybody," she said, handing around the autopsy report on Henry. Aside from the ticking of a clock, the only sound was an occasional gasp.

The autopsy showed that Henry had a massively enlarged, fatty liver. The spleen, ten times its normal size, had ruptured and bled profusely. The lymph nodes were severely swollen. There were harmful levels of lipids scattered all through his brain. The bone marrow, too, was full of fatty deposits. Even more horrifying, there was a cherry-red spot on the child's retina.

Ashlyn broke the silence. "Katy had a swollen spleen, too, but the doctors couldn't figure out why."

"Same with Jamie," said Peter, putting his arm around Josie, whose face had gone white. "But Jamie's doctors said he had neurofibromatosis."

A chorus of suddenly remembered symptoms tumbled out, things subtle and not-so-subtle that the parents had noticed as their babies had deteriorated. All three babies had had trouble feeding and had ultimately needed feeding tubes in the hospital. Nobody could recall any of the doctors saying anything about a red spot on the babies' retinas, but some of the other symptoms matched Henry's. Except when they didn't, like Jamie's odd skin lesions. Neither of the other two babies had those.

"Is it possible," David said finally, "that despite the different symptoms, all our babies died of the same thing? And at about the same age."

"But I wonder what it actually was," Sammie began. "Did the autopsy say what disease this was?"

They all flipped through the pages. Nothing. Just impenetrable medical jargon about lysosomal storage disease, mucolipidosis, mucopolysaccharidoses. On and on the impossible language of medicine went.

"If the pathologist couldn't name an actual disease, how can we?" moaned Josie.

"We need information," Peter said with urgency. "We need to know what these kids died of. And whether they all died of the same thing."

"Maybe there's some new virus or bacterium running rampant at Kramer's clinic," Sammie speculated. "Or maybe the lab has terrible infection control practices."

"But," countered Josie. "None of the other babies in our group have died."

"So, why did three babies die and not the others?" Sammie asked to nobody in particular.

A feeling of dark heaviness descended on the group, a crushing sense of the enormity of the task they were facing. Conversation ceased, shoulders sagged. Eventually, they realized it was getting late. The parents headed slowly out to their cars.

Bob and Sammie quietly put glasses in the dishwasher and untouched food in the fridge. A feeling of restlessness had settled over both of them throughout the evening. Finally, Sammie asked Bob whether he thought they could ever figure this out.

"I do have an idea," he said, putting his hands on her shoulders and looking her in the eye. "But it'll take both of us."

A WEEK LATER, Josie, Peter, Ashlyn, and the Steinbergs convened at Sammie and Bob's house again. But this time, the other women from Kramer's IVF seminar joined them. Bob and Sammie had been secretive about why they asked everybody to bring bottles, toys, and pacifiers from their babies. After the group had settled, Sammie plunged right in.

"I'm a reporter, not a scientist, as you all know," Sammie began, looking around at the curious faces. "But Bob, my husband here, is a molecular biologist, and so is Ashlyn, Katy's mom." She glanced at Ashlyn, whose gray face was a portrait of grief.

Sammie went on to explain that while neither Bob nor Ashlyn had specific expertise in infant diseases, they knew their way around different techniques for studying DNA.

"So that's why you wanted us to bring in all these bottles and toys?" asked one of the women from the IVF group.

"Exactly," interjected Ashlyn, finally coming to life a bit. She reached behind her chair and showed the group a big box of gallon-sized ziplock bags. She handed one to each woman.

"Put your child's toy or bottle in these, with your name on it and with the date of birth. We need to keep each child's DNA separate from the others."

The women dug into bags and purses and put their contributions into the ziplock bags.

"What are you going to do with all this?" one of the women asked.

Sammie jumped in again. The goal, she explained, was to compare all the samples of DNA and see where they differed. The hope was that there would be some detectable difference in the DNA of the babies who had died compared to the others.

She stressed that everything about this had to be kept confidential. They had to make sure not a word leaked out to anybody, especially anybody in Kramer's lab. She also decided not to tell the group that Bob and Ashlyn would do the DNA work at night secretly, in Bob's MIT lab. MIT would not be happy. But that was okay. For now.

17

APRIL 2019

The next morning, Sammie texted Jake Gordon at the *Times*.

"Hi, again," Sammie typed. "I'm beginning to put the pieces together on the death of the IVF babies. Can I come in to talk?"

To her surprise, Jake Gordon texted back right away.

"Can you come this afternoon? I've got some news, too."

Sammie texted the city desk at the *Daily* to say she had a family emergency, rushed home to change into better clothes, and drove straight to the *Times*. Jake's assistant spotted her as she entered the newsroom and waved hello. Minutes later,

Sammie was seated opposite Jake in his office. He got up and quietly closed the door.

"You first," Jake said, as usual, wasting no time.

"Okay. We now have three dead babies whose mothers got IVF at the same clinic, run by a guy named Dr. Saul Kramer. I've met with the grieving parents, as well as all the other women in their IVF group. All the other women have healthy babies," Sammie began.

Jake scribbled notes as Sammie talked.

"Here's the thing," she went on. She explained that she now had the full autopsy report on the third baby, who was born to a couple named David and Suzanne Steinberg. There had already been an autopsy on Jamie, the first baby. That autopsy had mentioned neurofibromatosis, which the parents already knew, but that shouldn't have been a cause of death. The autopsy on the third baby didn't even mention a specific disease. Some of the symptoms were the same in all three babies, like trouble swallowing, but not all. For instance, only the first baby had these dark skin spots. And the parents had shown no such symptoms themselves.

"Go on."

She did, explaining that she had started calling a few IVF clinics around the country, asking if they'd seen similar problems. She had been careful not to mention Dr. Saul Kramer by name. She also didn't mention anything specific about what might be happening at his lab.

"I've met Dr. Kramer and visited his lab, by the way," she added. "I was going to do a story on IVF, but I never got around to it." She described Kramer as a respected genetics researcher and reproductive endocrinologist, a real Harvard superstar.

She paused for breath, pleased to see that Jake seemed spellbound. Then she hit him with her best stuff: that she had collected DNA samples—saliva, mostly—from the toys and bottles of babies born to Dr. Kramer's patients, both from the babies who had died and the healthy ones.

She told him that her husband, Bob, and Ashlyn Wilson, the mother of one of the dead babies, were molecular biologists and were working together secretly in Bob's office to compare the DNA. In theory, they should be able to determine if there was anything different in the DNA of the babies who died.

Jake finally interrupted. "Let me get this straight. You think all the babies who died had the same disease?"

Sammie nodded.

"And you haven't told anybody about this? You haven't called the IVF clinic? Or the state health department? Wouldn't these deaths have sparked suspicion?"

"You'd think," Sammie agreed, "but no, not so far as I can tell."

"So, what do you need before we can dig into this more?" Jake asked.

"We?"

"Oh, yeah, I forgot to mention," Jake grinned. "I'm offering you a job. Obits. I got an okay this morning from the front office."

Sammie jumped up, barely squelching the urge to yell. Remembering she was a professional, and an adult, she quickly sat down again. Jake grinned.

"Wow! Thank you, thank you, Jake. Will I be able to work on this story in between obits?"

"I'm counting on it."

"When do I start?"

"How does Monday sound?"

"I should give the *Daily* a little notice," Sammie said. "How about a week from Monday?"

"Done," said Jake, getting up from his chair to shake her hand. "Welcome aboard."

Sammie floated out of the newsroom, texting Bob as she went. She was so excited that she didn't notice the black Jeep following her at a discreet distance as she exited the *Times* parking lot.

18

MAY 2019

On that fateful Monday morning, Sammie arrived early at the *Times*. She had gone in personally to the *Daily* to thank George Peabody for his support in the Joe Green mess, for giving her the statehouse job and, of course, to tell him about the offer from the *Times*.

"I'm going to take it," she told him, excited, but eager to be tactful and diplomatic. "I hate to say goodbye after all of your kindness to me, but I hope you understand."

Peabody, ever the Brahmin gentleman, understood perfectly. "I always knew we wouldn't be able to keep you for long," he had said as graciously as ever. "Don't be a stranger."

Now settling into her assigned spot in the cavernous *Times* newsroom, Sammie stashed her purse under her desk and sat impatiently as the *Times* tech guy helped her log into the newsroom computer system. She had already introduced herself to the telephone operators who sat in the center of the newsroom cheerfully fielding hundreds of calls a day from tipsters, complainers, and downright cranks.

As the newbie on obits, Sammie knew she'd be spending most of her time on the phone placating grieving families who insisted that their much-loved, but ordinary, relatives warranted an obit as much as somebody richer and more famous. It was hopeless, of course. Too many dead people, too few pages in the paper.

Sammie began sorting through the stack of potential obits, checking with funeral directors to make sure the person in question was actually dead, all too aware of the famous newsroom legend. A previous obit writer, no longer on staff, had written a glowing obit about a man who, it turned out, was not dead. The man's so-called friends had pulled off a colossal hoax, which the hapless reporter would, and should, have discovered had he bothered to contact the funeral home.

By 1 p.m., Sammie had cranked out two obits, eaten a sandwich at her desk, and pulled out her notes on IVF clinics. In spare moments at home last week, she had asked a spokesperson at each of the fifteen largest IVF clinics in the country if he or she knew of unusual deaths among infants born from IVF programs. She soon discovered that just like babies conceived naturally, babies born through IVF could die from many causes that involved no malfeasance at all: birth defects, preterm births, low birth weight, sudden infant death syndrome, bacterial infections, respiratory distress, neonatal hemorrhage, even accidents like suffocation, drowning, and falling from apartment windows.

But the good news, from the point of view of her developing story, was that none of the clinics reported unexplained deaths like those of Josie's, Ashlyn's, and the Steinbergs' babies.

JOSIE AND PETER had taken Sammie's gentle suggestion that they see a marriage counselor. It was easy to see they loved each other, but were stuck in their individual and joint grief. With each passing day, the distance between them seemed to grow. As a therapist herself, Josie knew they needed help and was eager to start. Peter took some convincing, but finally agreed.

On a cloudy Monday morning, they sat nervously in the office of their new therapist, a tall, lanky woman with short black hair and a penchant for loose, flowery blouses and flouncy pants. She had greeted them warmly at the door of her Cambridge office.

The office was simple but cozy, the walls chock full of photographs of animals and nature scenes. Settling themselves on the couch, Josie took the box of tissues from the coffee table and put it squarely between herself and Peter.

"We may need this," she said. Peter patted her on the shoulder gently, a kindness the therapist quietly scribbled on her notepad.

"So, maybe you should start from the beginning," the therapist said.

Finishing each other's sentences, Peter and Josie told the story of their roller-coaster IVF experience, the birth of Jamie and his mysterious death. They both cried. The therapist looked from one to the other, her face telegraphing empathy.

"So, basically, we're here because I want to try IVF again and Peter doesn't," said Josie, her voice conveying more desperation than anger at her husband.

"I just can't get my hopes up again," Peter admitted, fists clenched in his lap. "This whole thing is destroying our marriage. We're not actually fighting, but we're just in limbo."

"Have you thought about adoption?" the therapist asked.

"Yes," they said in unison. Josie added that their friend Ashlyn was considering adopting, though not right away since she was on her way back to Africa to resume her old research project.

"But I, we, I . . ." Josie couldn't finish the thought.

"I think I could maybe adopt," Peter offered tentatively, "but Josie really wants our own child."

Josie teared up again. The therapist put her pad down and looked them both in the eye. She took a deep breath and leaned forward.

"I don't know what the two of you will ultimately decide, and I certainly can't tell you what to do. But I can help you sort out your feelings on all this."

They sat again in silence, the weight of their sorrow pushing them deeper into the couch. Finally, Josie looked at her watch and caught Peter's eye. Time was always up in therapy just when psyches relaxed enough to let the pain come to the surface. As Josie reached for her purse, the therapist spoke again, looking them both in the eye.

"I want to compliment you both. The fact that you are willing to stay together and to come in here and sort this out is impressive. I admire your courage, individually and as a couple. I'm honored to help."

They rose, each thanking the therapist. Josie grabbed a final tissue and they headed for the door.

THAT NIGHT, IN a trailer park just outside Lowell, Joe Green sat barefoot in his baggy gym shorts and tank top, the open bottle of Jim Beam on the small table next to his laptop. He didn't bother with plastic cups anymore. Chugging straight from the bottle worked just fine.

After getting fired and crashing on his sister's couch until she kicked him out, he had spent a chunk of his pension from the *Daily* on a camper trailer. The trailer park he had found near Lowell had electricity, Wi-Fi, showers, mail delivery, and reasonable proximity to the fast-food joints that supplied him with his more than four thousand calories a day of grease and salt.

His growing belly rested on his thighs as he typed, but who the fuck cared? He was more or less homeless, unemployed, and had given up on AA, his sister, and all that other personal growth shit. All he wanted now was revenge on that Samantha Fuller bitch who had ratted him out in that gotcha interview in the *Daily* and wrecked what was left of his so-called life.

He didn't have a gun license and wouldn't have known how to fire one anyway. So, he searched online for alternatives, slugging away at the Jim Beam as he went. There it was. Perfect. Three hundred dollars. That would further dent his shrinking budget, but, hey, it would be worth it: a crossbow. And a manual to go with it. Granted, it wasn't a gun, but it could be just as lethal. He hadn't practiced archery since he was a kid in camp and, he remembered that he hadn't been very good at it then. But he could practice, off in the woods near the trailer camp. And unlike when he was in camp, this time he had serious motivation.

He read the description aloud. "Carbon express crossbow performance for the entry-level hunter. Single-piece, cast metal riser and extruded aluminum rail." He had no idea what that meant, but it sounded good and the picture on the web was awesome. "Adjustable butt stock and multi-position fore-grip for a customized fit—anti-dry-fire trigger."

"Holy shit," he mumbled, reaching for his wallet with the one remaining, almost maxed-out credit card. He ordered the lethal thing and finished off the whiskey.

19

MAY 2019

Bleary-eyed from lack of sleep, but energized by the late hours in the lab with Bob and Ashlyn the night before, Sammie slid into her desk at the *Times*, squeezed in a few investigative calls, and was about to switch over to obits when her cell dinged. A text from Bob.

"Call me. ASAP," he had written.

"What's up, honey?" Sammie called back right away, speaking quietly so nearby reporters couldn't hear. Curious heads around her popped up as they always did in the newsroom whenever a phone call suddenly went sotto voce.

"Can you get away at lunch and meet me and Ashlyn in the lab?" Bob asked.

Sammie glanced at the growing number of emails from funeral homes, potential obits for tomorrow's paper. "Sure," she said without hesitation. "What is it? Can you tell me now?"

"Not on the phone," he said.

An hour later, Bob, Ashlyn, and Sammie huddled over Bob's computer. To Sammie's untrained eye, there was just a string of A's, T's, G's, and C's on the screen. But Ashlyn and Bob leaned over and pointed excitedly.

"Right there, chromosome 11, the short arm," said Bob.

Sammie looked. "Yeah?"

"See those letters? That's the DNA from Josie's baby," said Ashlyn, pointing to the name "Jamie Northrup" at the bottom of the image.

Bob clicked to change the screen. "Now look at this."

Another string of letters, a different name. "That's my baby," said Ashlyn, choking up, even though she had seen the same thing earlier that morning. "That's my Katy."

Bob clicked again. "And here's the Steinbergs' baby."

"Let me guess. The same pattern of letters in the DNA?" Sammie said.

"Yup," said Bob. "All three babies had a mutation in the same place on chromosome 11."

"How do you know it's a mutation?" Sammie asked.

"Because of this," said Bob, unable to resist putting a note of drama in his voice when he said "this." He clicked again. This time, the screen showed a different sequence of the four letters.

"This is what this stretch of DNA, this gene, is supposed to look like. This is the image from one of the healthy babies."

Sammie was getting it, kind of. "So, all three babies who died had something wrong in the same gene in their DNA compared to the healthy babies, right?"

"Exactly," Ashlyn and Bob answered in unison.

"And that means . . ." Sammie said, waiting for one of them to complete her sentence.

"Most likely," Bob answered, "it means all three babies died of the same problem."

"But they all had different symptoms," mused Ashlyn.

"And that," continued Bob, "means that while they all may have died from this mutation, something else was going on, too."

They hovered again over Bob's computer. Bob gasped. Right there, on the short arm of chromosome 22, was something else that wasn't supposed to be there, something else in all three babies.

"This is really weird," Bob said, sitting back in his chair. Why were there two odd stretches of DNA in all three babies? Why did only Jamie have those skin spots and not the other two babies?

THE NEXT HURDLE was obviously to figure out what diseases or problems these odd genes caused, whether these diseases could explain the symptoms the three sick babies had, and, in some ways most important, whether the parents of these three babies were carriers for these diseases.

Sammie fell silent, then noticed that Ashlyn had walked away, sobbing quietly. Sammie walked over and put her arm around her shoulders.

"Did I give my baby a fatal disease?" Ashlyn choked. "Was it my fault?" Sammie tightened her hug.

"No," Bob intervened firmly, joining the two women. Even if she had been a carrier and even if her sperm donor was, too, he said, looking Ashlyn directly in the eye, it would still not be her fault. At worst, it would be her DNA, not her.

"So, what do we do next?" Sammie asked, her arm still protectively around Ashlyn's shoulders.

Easy, Bob said. Now they had to test all the parents—Ashlyn, her sperm donor, Josie, Peter, and the Steinbergs to see if they had this odd, mutant DNA. If, for instance, both Josie and Peter had one copy of the mutant gene, that would explain why Jamie had the disease. The same with the other parents. "This is getting very real," Sammie said, her stomach in knots. "Are we in over our heads here?"

"No," answered Bob, "but somebody might be."

THAT AFTERNOON, AS Sammie went back to obits, Bob emailed the mutant DNA sequences from chromosome 11 and chromosome 22 from the three dead babies to one of the country's largest DNA databases. He had only one question: What diseases, if any, do these genes code for?

That evening, Bob and Sammie gathered the IVF group once again at their house. Liam and Beau had been lured to bed early with the promise of extra video-game time.

Sammie had ordered pizza, and the scent of oregano filled the house. In the living room, someone opened one of the big boxes and everyone began sliding the hot, gooey slices onto paper plates.

"Wait, before you put anything in your mouths," Bob spoke up loudly. "Stop a second."

Everybody looked up. Bob passed out the saliva swab kits and asked each of the parents to swab the inside of their cheeks, insert the swab into a small sterile container, and write their names on the label. With a minimum of chatter, Josie, Peter, Ashlyn, the Steinbergs and the others dutifully swabbed their cheeks, then reached for their wine.

Ashlyn, still visibly upset from seeing little Katy's DNA on the computer earlier, spoke quietly. "I called the clinic where I got my donor sperm. They're going to send me another sample so we can check my donor's DNA."

The mood was cautiously optimistic. At the very least, the grieving parents might be able to finally understand what happened, and the other parents from the original IVF group might be able to rest assured that their babies were safe. For once, they chatted about other things.

After they'd left, Bob cleaned up the kitchen, while Sammie looked in on Liam and Beau. Both boys were asleep, earbuds still connected. She gently took the earbuds out of each boy's ears and tucked her babies in. Bob poked his head in the doorway, catching her eye.

"They're so precious," Sammie whispered to him. "I can't imagine losing a child."

IT WAS ANOTHER late night for Kramer. He was, thankfully, alone in the lab. Ricardo had not bumbled in again since the night he had come back for his cell phone. Manuel, the janitor, had come and gone.

Kramer took advantage of the solitude to go over his records. He counted slowly and carefully. Five babies so far born with the Niemann-Pick gene, three already dead. Seven more pregnancies established and going well. If all went according to plan, before long he could claim twelve infant deaths from his lethal work. He wasn't winning, exactly. But he was ever so slowly evening the score: Nazis, millions; Kramer, almost twelve. If he could scale up fast, maybe he could get to 100. Maybe even more.

A long way to go, but Kramer, to his great relief, was finding it relatively easy, thanks to patient advocacy groups, to find families with children afflicted with Niemann-Pick and get them to send him DNA samples. From there, he could easily extract the deadly gene. And, as far as he could tell, Ricardo and Heather still didn't suspect a thing, even when the supply of the mutant genes ran low. Even better, Ellen had stopped complaining about his late nights in the lab. Things were really looking up. And adding that MSH2 decoy gene had been a brilliant move, he congratulated himself. That gene could wreak havoc all over the genome, creating endless mutations, maybe even some new diseases. No one would ever figure out what he was doing.

Satisfied, Kramer shut off the light as he left the lab and stopped by his office to get his keys and briefcase. He paused when he spotted the silver-framed picture of Isaiah he brought from home to keep on his desk here. He picked it up, brought it to his lips, and kissed it.

"Your death will not go unavenged, little Isaiah," he said aloud. "Daddy is seeing to that."

A FEW DAYS later, Bob opened his computer and to his delight, spotted the email he had been waiting for. It was from the data bank. They had identified the DNA samples he had sent.

"Bingo!" he whispered to himself. One was a disease gene. Something called Niemann-Pick. He had never heard of it, but it was a real gene. The other, the DNA from chromosome 22, was even weirder—a gene called MSH2. In some cases, he read, mutations in this MSH2 gene were linked to a condition called Constitutional Mismatch Repair Deficiency, or CMMRD. Good Lord! He kept reading.

"Oh, my God," he whispered to himself. "This MSH2 gene can cause changes in skin coloring similar to those caused with neurofibromatosis."

"Jamie!" he realized. That's what Jamie was diagnosed with. The doctors thought he had neurofibromatosis. In fact, it was really this MSH2 gene. And if this MSH2 gene really causes mutations all over the place, it could have caused different symptoms, or even no symptoms, in the other babies. Niemann-Pick would have actually killed the babies, but MSH2 would have thrown their doctors completely off track. Holy shit.

He texted Sammie. "Can you come over to the lab? Now?"

"Hold on," she texted back, glancing over to the editor's office. "Let me ask Jake."

Sammie strolled as casually as she could to Jake's corner office and waited until he put down his phone. Sammie raised her eyebrows. He waved her in.

"We're getting something," she said as she sank into a chair. Other reporters had noticed the unusual rapport Sammie seemed to have with the boss, especially since she was still so new.

"Bob thinks he's found the gene that caused the babies' deaths," Sammie rushed on. "The babies who died all had a mutation that the healthy babies don't. He found another weird gene, too, just in the babies who died."

Jake twirled a pencil around his right forefinger and thumb. "Okay, so, what does that tell us? It could still be bad luck, couldn't it? Coincidence?"

"That's what we're trying to figure out. Bob wants me to go over to his lab right now, but I've got this whole stack of obits. . . ."

"Go. Now," said Jake. "And Sammie? Be careful. Not a word to anybody."

SAMMIE MET ASHLYN going into Bob's lab. Ashlyn looked better today, still sad, but her eyes were bright now with the excitement of any scientist on the hunt. Sammie couldn't help thinking how similar it was to a reporter on the trail of a great story.

"We got it," said Bob, trying to keep his voice low. "That first strange DNA sequence, from chromosome 11, is the gene for a fatal disease called Niemann-Pick."

Sammie quickly unzipped her laptop case and logged on, Googling "Niemann-Pick." She began reading the symptoms out loud: enlarged spleen and enlarged, fatty liver, swollen lymph nodes, high lipid levels in the brain. On and on went the dismal list.

"That's it," said Ashlyn. "That's what the Steinbergs' baby had. And some of those things, my baby and Josie's may have had toward the end. But how on earth . . ."

"That's why we tested all the parents. We have to know if they passed these genes to their babies," said Bob excitedly. He turned back to his computer.

"Now, look at this," he said, as Ashlyn and Sammie leaned over his shoulder. "The parents' saliva test results. They just came in, too."

They all held their breath as Bob scrolled through the mass of A's, T's, G's, and C's on the screen, mumbling words Sammie couldn't catch and wouldn't have understood anyway.

For Sammie, the minutes ticked by agonizingly. Science still felt like magic, a world that some people lived in and others didn't. She didn't. She felt, by turns, stupid and awestruck, simultaneously left out of and, for brief seconds, let into a mysterious puzzle.

At last, Bob and Ashlyn straightened up. Bob looked at Sammie, his face alight.

"Not a single one, none of the parents carries the Niemann-Pick gene, not even Ashlyn's sperm donor. And nobody carries this other gene, either," he said. "There's no way these babies could have gotten these genes from their parents. That leaves . . ."

"The IVF clinic," Sammie said, excited. "It has to be."

"So, it really isn't my fault," Ashlyn exhaled. Her voice filled with gratitude and an overwhelming sense of relief. "Which means it has to be somebody at the lab." Maybe, she mused, they mixed up the parents or something while they were fertilizing the eggs. Maybe she got some other father's DNA? For some reason, that thought horrified her almost more than the fear that her own genes had contributed to her child's death.

"Your donor was clearly the father," corrected Bob. "Neither of you carried these genes."

"So, how . . ." Ashlyn's voice trailed off.

Sammie went still, then spoke softly.

"I have to tell Jake."

As SAMMIE RUSHED off to make her call, Ashlyn and Bob looked at each other. Ashlyn wanted to call all the parents to tell them what they had found. Bob wasn't so sure.

So far, all they knew was that something had happened at the IVF clinic to give these babies the lethal Niemann-Pick gene and this mutation accelerator gene. But they didn't have absolute proof yet. Someone had done this, yes, but who? And why? If they told the parents, the secrecy of their investigation could be compromised. If they didn't, they would be leaving the parents with the agony of uncertainty. And who should they tell? Just the parents of the three dead babies? Or all the parents from the IVF group? The more people they told, the bigger the chances that word would leak out too soon.

Ashlyn decided to make the calls, just to Josie and Peter and the Steinbergs. She would swear them to secrecy until Sammie finished her investigation. It was unfair, she and Bob concluded, for them to know and not the others. Ashlyn went first to Josie and Peter's condo. Josie could tell from her friend's face that she had serious news.

"Tell us, Ashlyn. Please," she urged. She and Peter settled on the couch, holding hands. Ashlyn sat in the big chair facing the couch.

"It was no accident," Ashlyn began. "A lethal gene for a disease called Niemann-Pick was inserted into our fertilized eggs at the IVF clinic." It has to be, she went on. Neither of them was a carrier for this. Ashlyn wasn't, either, nor was her donor. This was no accident. Their babies were murdered. Ashlyn's voice shook but her eyes were steely. She also told them about the MSH2 gene, the gene that most likely caused the skin changes in Jamie that their doctors attributed to neurofibromatosis.

"Jamie, Katy, and little Henry all died of this horrible thing," she said, wound up now. "We have no idea why our babies were killed and none of the other women's were.

Someone did this to us. Just to us. For some god-awful . . ." Ashlyn couldn't finish, sobbing so hard suddenly that she had trouble catching her breath.

Josie and Peter, tears streaming down both their faces, got up off the couch and hugged Ashlyn. The three grieving parents stayed like that for a long time. Finally, Ashlyn broke away from the hug. "I still have to tell the Steinbergs," she said.

"We'll come with you," said Peter.

The Steinbergs met them at the door, stony-faced, almost physically bracing themselves for whatever news they were about to hear.

The five sat down in the living room. The couple said nothing as Ashlyn repeated what she and Bob had discovered. The room was deadly quiet. David stared at the floor, and his wife held her face in her hands. Finally, she looked up.

"Thank you," she said. "For doing this and for telling us. Could you all please go now?"

Silently, they did.

20

JUNE 2019

Sammie worked the phones hard. All day, every day. She called IVF experts all over the world, learning the intricacies of IVF procedures. She combed the scientific journals, read blogs, cruised medical websites. She was on a mission, determined to learn as much as she could.

Soon, it became clear to her that the key moment in all the manipulations of sperm and eggs was when a new gene could be secretly inserted into the embryo during the preimplantation screening, that final check of the chromosomes before it was transplanted into the uterus of the prospective mother.

"How hard would it be to tamper with an embryo at this stage? How hard would it be to take out one gene and insert another?" Sammie asked expert after expert. Easy, they said, reminding her of the basic process—that after an egg is fertilized, it develops into a blastocyst, which then becomes an embryo and implants into the uterus.

"Could this tampering be done in secret?"

The experts were unanimous and, to her relief, willing to be quoted by name. On the record. As long as the geneticist was alone in the lab, they told her, it would almost be child's play. No one would know anything had been tampered with until much later. In fact, they emphasized, this was the whole point of the new CRISPR technology—to pause at that key moment in the process and take out a bad gene and replace it with a healthy one.

"And would it be possible to do the reverse, take out a healthy gene and insert a bad one?" Sammie always held her breath when she asked this question.

"Of course," the experts had all said. "But who would do that?"

That was, indeed, the question, which led to an even more urgent question: Whoever it was, could he or she be stopped before more babies were doomed to die? Sammie's heart pounded. How much time did she have? How many potential embryos had already been tampered with? How many more were in process?

It was time to call Kramer. Sammie took a deep breath and made the call.

JOSIE AND PETER went several more times to their marriage counselor. Under her gentle nudging, Peter was able to empathize with Josie's deep desire to try IVF one more time. For her part, Josie managed to relax her anxiety enough to understand the depth of Peter's reluctance, even acknowledging her own misgivings about plunging into IVF all over again.

But eventually, they had come together, agreeing to go to a new clinic and try just one more IVF cycle. They knew from what Bob and Ashlyn had told them that something had gone drastically wrong at Kramer's clinic, even if they didn't know exactly what. They had no desire to see Kramer ever again. And if IVF in a new clinic didn't work, they agreed, they would give up and take stock of their lives. They agreed to leave the adoption option open.

A week after their decision, they sat facing a young reproductive endocrinologist at an IVF clinic two hours away in Connecticut. To their surprise, gone were their nerves, their anxiety. They were old hands at this IVF business now, and eager to get started.

Their story stunned the doctor, who admitted she was stumped as to why two people, neither of whom carried the gene for Niemann-Pick disease, could have produced a baby with the deadly disease. The doctor, loyal as most doctors are to their tribe, had been careful not to lay blame directly on Kramer's clinic, though her facial cues suggested she had some serious concerns.

"I'm so sorry," she said diplomatically. "But I'm glad you're trying again here." The doctor noted that her clinic had done its own tests earlier that morning, confirming that neither Josie nor Peter carried the mutant Niemann-Pick gene. "It's safe for you to try again," she assured them.

Before they left, Peter produced another sperm sample, and Josie filled the prescriptions for the hormones she would need to take. In the car on the way home, they called Ashlyn, who answered the phone breathlessly.

"I'm packing. What a nightmare," Ashlyn sighed into the phone. She wanted nothing more to do with IVF, Boston, or babies. All she wanted was to get as far away as she could. To her great relief, she had been able to rejoin her old research team and, in a few days, would be headed to Kenya to study malaria again. Before Katy, Ashlyn's research was her passion. She needed that again, to feel good about something, anything, again.

If she couldn't create a new life, maybe she could at least help develop a vaccine or maybe even a cure for malaria and save millions of lives. Still, she was thrilled that Josie and Peter were trying again. She told them how happy she was for them, but also wondered how they had the strength to go through with it again. She kept those thoughts to herself.

"We just saw the doctor at the new clinic," Josie reported, smiling at Peter, who was driving. "Just one cycle. That's our agreement. If that fails, maybe we'll quit our jobs and join you in Africa."

Ashlyn laughed. "Anytime, you guys, anytime."

A WEEK LATER, Sammie flopped back in her chair around 10 p.m., the newsroom quiet, her fourth coffee of the day finally wearing off. She yawned and stretched her arms and legs luxuriantly, viscerally aware that she hadn't run for days and hadn't done yoga for a month. She suddenly noticed that she was hungry, too, having forgotten both lunch and dinner. She reached for a protein bar in her top desk drawer.

Except for the old hands at the night desk, Sammie was alone in the newsroom. Bob had put the kids to bed and had just called, urging her to knock off for the night and come home.

"Soon," Sammie told him. "I'm almost out the door."

Reaching for her purse, Sammie felt satisfied. The hard reporting was done, the interviews finished, her notes in order. Her story was budgeted for Page One on Sunday. Jake had given her as much space as she wanted. The planned layout looked spectacular.

The photo department had dug up old file photos of Dr. Saul Kramer—giving speeches, showing off his lab—always looking very Harvard. A *Times* photographer had also managed, unobtrusively, to snap shots of him getting out of his car and going in the door of his clinic. Josie, Peter, Ashlyn, and the Steinbergs had willingly had their photos taken, too, as had the entire IVF group, the happy moms lined up holding their toddlers in their arms. The *Times* had opted, for reasons of compassion and delicacy, to run the photos of the babies who died inside, not on Page One.

The graphics department had come through, too, with help from Bob and Ashlyn, who put together diagrams showing the various steps of IVF treatment. The *Times* team had also found great diagrams of how CRISPR works. It still amazed Sammie all that they had learned on this journey. They knew the what and the how. Now, the question on all their minds was the why.

Altogether, there were four full pages of art and diagrams, with Sammie's intro on the top of the front page, above the fold, and the "jumps" laid out for three more pages, all in the main section of the *Times*. All that was left was to write the thing, make it sing, and not get sued. The *Times* lawyers were on call to read the piece as soon as Sammie finished writing it.

She waved to the night desk folks and walked out to her car. She was exhausted, but more excited than she had been in a long time. She turned on the ignition, silenced the radio, and drove out of the *Times* lot.

Weird, she thought, glancing in her rearview mirror and noticing the headlights behind her. She had thought she was the only reporter still in the newsroom. Well, maybe it was just a photographer heading to a fire or something.

As Sammie swung onto the highway, the headlights stayed with her, but her mind was elsewhere, already working on the lede for her story.

21

JULY 2019

That Sunday, Sammie's story took up most of Page One. It read:

At least three babies born recently after their parents sought treatment at a Boston-area in vitro fertilization clinic died after their embryos were apparently altered with the new gene-editing technique called CRISPR.

According to private laboratory research commissioned by the Times, the results of which have not been published in a peer-reviewed, scientific journal, the tampered embryos contained genes for a deadly, inherited disease called Niemann-Pick. The tampered embryos also contained a gene that increases the mutation rate in general, which triggered odd symptoms that for months had thrown the babies' pediatricians off track.

The Niemann-Pick gene controls an enzyme that, when missing or mutated, causes lipids to build up in an infant's body over the course of about a year, eventually leading to unavoidable death. None of the parents of the three deceased children carried the deadly gene, which is most common in Ashkenazi Jews. The fact that none of the parents carry the gene means that the deadly gene must have been introduced into the embryos artificially.

This is the first known incident of deaths apparently induced by CRISPR, widely touted as a potential cure for genetic diseases but also feared by ethicists and others as a method with the potential to cause harm and, in theory, change some of the genetics of the human race. CRISPR stands for "clustered regularly interspaced short palindromic repeats."

Medical ethicists contacted by the Times *and several leading Congressmen expressed outrage and vowed to increase pressure to ban CRISPR research on human fertilized eggs and embryos. Spokespersons for a number of advocacy groups for people with inherited diseases urged caution in banning potentially beneficial research. Scientists currently working with CRISPR similarly stressed its potential for good, arguing that curtailing research because of apparent wrongdoing in one lab was not justified.*

Reached yesterday for comment, the Harvard-trained chief of the clinic, Dr. Saul Kramer, denied any malfeasance and provided a written statement. Kramer holds an MD degree from Harvard Medical School and a PhD from MIT in genetics and reproductive endocrinology.

"Our clinic has long been one of the leading IVF research centers in the nation," the statement said. "Our practice maintains the highest professional and ethical standards. Our work has led to the births

of hundreds of healthy babies over many years. We are devastated to learn that three babies from our clinic have died. We have no information about what may have caused their deaths. Tragically, some infants die in the first year of life, whether they are conceived via IVF or normally. Our hearts go out to the families of these infants."

The Massachusetts Department of Public Health, alerted to the deaths late last week by the Times, said it would look into the clinic, adding that it had no previous knowledge of the situation. A department spokeswoman said the state has had no complaints about the clinic until now. Other state officials said the clinic's license was in order and that Dr. Saul Kramer is in good standing with the board of registration in medicine and has had no malpractice suits filed against him.

Ms. Josie Reimann Northrup, a psychotherapist and mother of one of the deceased infants, said in an interview, "It was agony watching our little boy die slowly, getting worse week by week." She noted that he could barely move at the end, and was on a feeding tube. "We had been so thrilled to have him," she told the Times. "We had been trying for a long time. We believe our son's death was premeditated murder."

Her husband, Peter Northrup, a lawyer, was emphatic. "This is not just malpractice. It is not a random event that could have happened to anybody. This was a deliberate effort to introduce a lethal gene into an otherwise healthy fertilized egg." Northrup declined to comment on whether the parents of the deceased children planned to sue the clinic.

Ms. Ashlyn Wilson, a molecular biologist and also the mother of a deceased baby, said, "The Northrups and I were part of a group of parents treated at the same time in Dr. Kramer's clinic. My baby and theirs were the only ones in our group to die. All the other babies were healthy. Why not ours?"

Wilson, along with Bob Brightman, an MIT molecular biolo-gist conducted genetic research on the DNA of the deceased infants, their parents, and the healthy babies at the request of the Times. *The research was conducted at MIT. (Full disclosure: Bob Brightman is this reporter's husband. His research on this was paid for by the* Times.)

A spokesman for MIT said he was not aware of this research and did not condone it, adding that top administrators were consid-ering a paid leave of absence for Brightman.

Suzanne and David Steinberg also had an infant son who died after the couple went through IVF treatment at the Kramer clinic. The autopsy found their child had classic symptoms of Niemann-Pick, including an enlarged liver and spleen, swollen lymph nodes, and lipid deposits in the brain and bone marrow. The baby also had a cherry-red spot on his retinas.

Some of those symptoms were identical to the ones suffered by Wilson's and the Northrups' babies.

The story continued on the inside pages of the *Times* to explain how CRISPR works, standard IVF procedures, and comments from numerous scientists unconnected to the Boston clinic. All stated that there would be no way, short of deliberate interference, that three babies from the same clinic would acquire a deadly gene that their parents did not carry.

22

JULY 2019

Until moments ago, Ricardo was feeling grateful for a day home from work and the lab. Now, he threw down the *Times* and staggered to the kitchen sink, just in time to vomit violently. He gasped, vomited again, then, knees buckling, slid to the floor in sobs. His wife, their baby on her hip, heard the commotion and came rushing in.

"Ricardo, what happened? What's wrong?"

Ricardo writhed on the floor, unable to speak, barely able to breathe. Finally, he raised an arm to point to the counter and gasped, "the paper, the *Times,* right there."

His wife, Melanie, sat on the high stool at the counter, jiggled the baby absentmindedly on her lap, and picked up the paper. "Oh my God. Oh my God," she exhaled as she read. "Oh, no. No, no, no!"

She glanced down to the floor where Ricardo now lay silent, eyes closed, his whole body shaking.

"I can't believe this," she said. "This is Kramer, isn't it? This is Kramer's doing."

Ricardo's cell phone rang from the counter. Recognizing the name on the phone, Melanie answered for him.

"Heather, I know. We just read it," Melanie said, still staring at the paper.

In the kitchen of her Brookline mansion, Ellen Kramer poured herself coffee and buttered a bagel, barely registering that Saul wasn't there. He had been doing so many all-nighters lately, she was used to having breakfast alone. She picked up the paper, took one look and fainted, crumpling to the floor.

Dr. Saul Kramer didn't need to see the paper to know what was hitting the fan. Ever since that reporter, Samantha Somebody, had called him for comment on Friday, he had known what was coming. He had not slept since that interview, despite adding Ambien to his Klonopin and Xanax. He had given his entire lab staff the weekend off, telling them in no uncertain terms that he wanted the lab to himself. Ricardo and Heather had glanced at each other and raised their eyebrows but said nothing.

Friday night, after the call from the *Times*, he had worked like a demon, grimly thrilled to have ten more fertilized eggs lined up for preimplantation screening, five of which, he had determined, were the eggs of couples with German heritage. He quickly checked the other five and okayed them for implantation.

He put the five to be tampered with on the counter. He gathered his materials, including the CRISPR kit containing the deadly Niemann-Pick gene. He had his technique down to an art form by now. He took out the healthy gene from each of the "German" fertilized eggs and inserted the lethal one in its place.

He kept at it all day Saturday and Saturday night. It was a race against the clock now. When the *Times* story hit, who knew what would happen? Would the cops come immediately? Would the issue be batted about in the news for a while first? Would his patients start freaking out?

By early Sunday morning, he had worked on a dozen more fertilized eggs, getting sloppier in his haste with each one. Used syringes lay scattered on the counter, safe medical practices gone to hell. There was one syringe left containing the deadly Niemann-Pick gene. He picked it up and stared at it for a long moment, deciding.

A few minutes later, he heard the Sunday *Times* thump against the front door of the clinic. He shut off the lights in the lab, stopped by his office, and put the picture of little Isaiah in his briefcase along with his white coat, then headed outside. He did not go to his car. It would be too easy to track the license plate. Instead, he grabbed the bike he sometimes rode to work and rode away. He did not go home.

ELLEN KRAMER CAME to on her kitchen floor, coffee spilled, her bagel lying on the floor next to her. She rose up on one elbow, then slowly got to her knees, bracing herself on a chair, and stood up. Her head throbbed from hitting the counter, then the floor as she fell, but she didn't think she had a concussion. Being married to a doctor for so long, self-diagnosis had become natural.

In fact, her thoughts were clearer than they had been in years. She knew it at once, felt it in her bones: Her husband was a murderer.

She should have known. He had had some weird kind of energy lately, almost maniacal, but she had tuned it out. She sat down and made herself read the entire *Times* story slowly, gagging on her own bile, but determined to absorb every horrible detail. She called her children, hoping to warn them before they read the paper. All she got was their voice mail. She promised to call again in a few hours.

They would all need each other now, the remnants of this devastated family. Would the kids want to see their father? She hoped not. Would they believe the newspaper story? She guessed they would.

She gathered up the newspaper and, tucking it under her arm, went upstairs to her study. She was on autopilot now, remembering who she used to be before years of marriage to an apparent monster. She walked over to her safe and spun the dial on the lock. She hastily removed her jewelry, passport, birth certificate, and the birth certificates of the children, including Isaiah's, the deed to their house, and all the other papers she deemed important. She picked up her checkbooks, both her laptop and Saul's, and called the emergency number for a locksmith.

Ignoring the constant beeps from her cell and landline, she packed her car with as many clothes and belongings as she could gather. When the locksmith arrived, she watched closely as he changed the locks on all the doors. She paid him in cash, then changed the code on the garage and the security alarm. She set the security alarm, jotting down the new number in a notebook that she stashed in her purse.

Once in her car, she called her lawyer and asked for an emergency meeting later in the day. She told him she wanted to start divorce proceedings and needed a restraining order immediately. Baffled, he had asked a string of questions that she cut off with a brusque, "Later. Please." In the face of complete and utter devastation, Ellen Kramer seemed to find her long-lost strength.

Ellen then drove to the Brookline police station, where she startled a cop at the front desk.

"My husband is a mass murderer," she blurted, handing over Saul's laptop. "I know he did it."

She thrust her copy of the *Times* at the officer and walked unsteadily to the bench.

He radioed for his supervisor and sat down beside her.

"Please follow me. You'll be more comfortable in here," the supervisor said, leading her down a narrow hallway with doors on either side, corkboards and police flyers strewn in between. Once they entered the room, Ellen sat quietly in one of the two chairs there. The supervisor sat opposite her and placed a digital recorder on the table between them. "Do you mind if I record this?" the officer asked.

"No," answered Ellen.

EVERYBODY EXCEPT ASHLYN Wilson, who had already flown back to Africa, showed up spontaneously at Sammie and Bob's house well before noon.

Josie and Peter were there, of course, along with the whole IVF group. Sammie's new friends from the *Times* dropped over as well, as did their neighbors, Sammie's parents, even the parents of Liam's and Beau's friends.

Many came with food, beer, and copies of the *Times*. Several had stopped at newsstands to buy extra copies. The TV crews began to arrive, too, delighted to find not just the newly famous Samantha Fuller, but IVF moms willing to be interviewed, as well as Bob, who, though a bit overwhelmed, was willing to explain the mechanics of CRISPR over and over to TV reporters, most of whom hadn't had a science class in years.

"What's happening, Mom? Is this a party?" Beau tugged on Sammie's sleeve as the house filled up. He and Liam had known she was on to some big story, but then again, in their eyes, their mom was always on to some big story.

Last night, she had sat them down to explain this new story to them, but they didn't really get it. All they understood was that there was a bad doctor out there somewhere who made babies die. And now, suddenly, their living room was full of excited people and TV cameras and their mother was one minute tearful, the next smiling. They escaped to their room; the one place that still seemed normal.

Even Sammie didn't know quite what to feel. Suddenly, it was all very real—the enormity of what Saul Kramer had done, and the uncertainty that still remained. What if she had gotten it all wrong? What if no one was to blame and it was all some kind of awful accident in the lab? Had she been fair? And now, she herself was the story. And the TV cameras. Her hair was a mess. She hadn't even showered yet.

Sammie begged Bob to stall the TV people until she could put herself together. She beckoned Josie to accompany her into the bathroom. Josie sat on the closed toilet seat, chatting with her over the sound of the shower, then watched as Sammie dressed, blow-dried her hair, and put on her mascara.

"You did it, Sammie, you did it," Josie beamed. She had, of course, wanted none of all this. But once she and Ashlyn and Sammie had begun to put the pieces together, she had become increasingly confident that her baby's death was no accident. Nothing could bring Jamie back, but nailing the bastard who did it would help a little.

"You got it right, Sammie. Take some deep breaths. You're a star, and you deserve to be."

"I'm not used to being the center of attention. I like to hide behind my byline," Sammie confessed. "I hope I got everything right."

"You did, Sammie. You know you did. I know you did," said Josie, gently nudging her out to the living room to face the cameras.

23

R icardo and Heather raced over to the lab, pushing their
way past a growing mob of reporters and a handful of
desperate IVF patients wanting to get inside to find out if their
precious embryos were safe.

Elbowing their way past the crowd and declining comment,
they hurriedly closed the door behind them. Inside, the clinic's
public relations officer looked up as they came in, his face that
of a hunted animal.

"This is a fucking nightmare," he yelled, his landline and
cell buzzing relentlessly, the fax machine spewing paper onto
the floor. "Where the hell is Kramer? Have you seen the lab?
It's a mess!"

Not stopping to commiserate, Ricardo and Heather hurried past.

"Just put out some mealymouthed statement that the clinic is investigating, that Kramer's whereabouts are unknown, and that all current IVF patients will be well taken care of," Ricardo said, then yelled over his shoulder, "Good luck."

Heather was already at the door of the lab, Ricardo close on her heels.

"Oh, my God," she said, opening the door. "Look at this." Used syringes lay all over the counter. The freezer was full of embryos marked ready for implantation. One lone syringe, slightly tinged with blood, lay on the floor.

"We have to destroy these embryos," said Ricardo. "He may have tampered with them."

"Are you crazy? We *can't* destroy them," Heather shot back, still crouched by the freezer. "They're evidence. We could get charged with murder."

"Then what the hell do we do with them?" Ricardo answered, roaming around the lab, looking in drawers and cabinets as if he could find clues there. "And what do we tell all those parents who think they're about to get pregnant?"

They looked at each other.

"We helped him do this, Ricardo. We're accomplices," Heather observed, eyes flaring. "We should have suspected something. We allowed this to happen."

"We didn't know what he was up to," Ricardo sighed, sinking into a nearby chair. "He did act weird that night I came back for my cell phone. But I thought he was just working late. Besides, he was always weird."

"Should we clean up this mess?" Heather asked.

"No," said Ricardo. "It's a crime scene now."

THE BROOKLINE POLICE station came quickly to life after Ellen Kramer's dramatic entrance. The officer on Sunday desk duty had called in his supervisor's supervisor, who had already read the *Times* story. Ellen's lawyer, Josh Smith, arrived, looking a bit hungover and confused, but ready to file a restraining order against Kramer. Kramer hadn't been violent to his wife, but if he could cold-bloodedly kill babies, he could certainly kill her.

At Smith's urging, the police called the judge on emergency duty. A temporary restraining order was approved within the hour. They would then have to go to court the following day to get the restraining order extended for another ten days.

Through it all, Ellen sat stone-faced. To her surprise, she felt no ambivalence. There was no love left for her husband. The *Times* story had rung true, though why Saul would do this, she could not begin to understand.

What she finally did know in her bones was that she had been married for decades to a stranger, a psychopath, and now, probably, a murderer. She had borne this man four children, three living, one dead. Yet all she felt right now was disgust and betrayal. He had been different lately, more edgy, more hostile. But wasn't that normal for a high-stress academic job? How was she supposed to know? Her thoughts rambled through her head like an unstoppable train, as she tried to make sense of what was happening.

After an hour, Ellen and Josh Smith left the police station for his office to begin preparing divorce papers. As she followed him in her car, she put her cell on Bluetooth to call her children. She found, not surprisingly, that they were in varying degrees of shock.

They had all read the *Times* story and peppered her with questions. Was she okay? Did she think the story was true? Had she noticed anything strange about him? Why would their seemingly normal father do such a thing? Where was he now? What should they do if he tried to contact any of them? Their thoughts mirrored hers.

"I'm okay, more or less," she told each of her children, her voice higher pitched than normal, but her words coldly coherent. "So, listen. Don't answer his calls or texts. Don't let him in the door. Don't talk to the press. I'll get you a lawyer if the press bothers you." She paused for breath, somewhat in shock about her newly discovered fortitude and resolve. Vaguely, and somewhat ironically, she wondered when the last time was that she had felt so strong, so clearheaded, knowing exactly what needed to be done and what steps had to be taken.

She told them that she had changed the locks, taken out a restraining order, and that she was going to a hotel tonight, stressing, as she did so, that, for the moment, she wanted to be alone. She added that she would probably go to their house on the Cape in the morning and asked them all to come. Her voice didn't shake as she told her children she was filing for divorce. She reassured them all that she was okay.

"We'll get through this together," she finished.

LATER THAT NIGHT, after leaving Bob and the kids with two large pizzas for dinner, Sammie headed back to the newsroom. She had spent a good part of the afternoon interviewing the crowd at the clinic, especially the distraught IVF patients, and had tried multiple times, to no avail, to interview the besieged clinic PR guy. All he had done was fax her the same tepid statement he gave to all the other news organizations.

When she had stopped by the Brookline police department, the officers told her they had put out an order for Kramer's arrest and that a judge had issued search warrants for the clinic and Kramer's home. When Sammie had stopped by Kramer's house, the place was swarming with cops. It appeared that no one was home.

Now, back at her desk, she wrote a quick update for tomorrow's paper based on her afternoon's reporting and organized her notes for tomorrow's calls: lawyers, more CRISPR experts, the state public health department. She listened to her dozens of phone messages and read dozens of emails, including, to her dismay, four from parents whose babies had also died after IVF at Kramer's clinic. She had always hoped that there were no others, but deep down, her reporter's instincts knew otherwise.

Finally, she texted Bob that she was on her way home.

As she exited the *Times* newsroom and headed for the parking lot, she never saw the black Jeep parked at a ninety-degree angle to the exit door with the driver's-side window rolled down. She never heard the *whoosh* of the arrow, either. All she felt was a sudden searing pain in her left thigh as the arrow found its mark.

As if from far away, she heard her own screams. For a brief moment before she passed out, Sammie caught a glimpse of a black Jeep screeching away. She thought she heard a familiar male voice yelling, "Fuck you, bitch."

THE STORY OF the attack on Sammie made the front page the next morning, written by Jake Gordon himself. While the timing of the attack, on the evening of her blockbuster piece, was suspicious, Gordon danced that fine journalistic line, careful not to suggest that Dr. Saul Kramer, the target of her stories, was a suspect in the attack. He did, however, mention prominently that there was a warrant out for Kramer's arrest. He also noted that the police had taken the arrow, retrieved from Sammie's leg, for fingerprinting and other forensic analysis.

Gordon immediately recruited his troops—four reporters to do follow-ups: One to "doorstep" the IVF clinic, that is, to hang around in hopes of interviewing an entering or exiting staff member. Another reporter, the science writer, was dispatched to CRISPR duty, to call scientists, ethicists, and policy makers about the pros and cons of tighter regulations on human embryo research. The third was the habitually grumpy general assignment reporter known as "Sparky" for his love of fires. Widely viewed as an old-timer, he came to life when told he could skip monitoring the police radio and do a "ride-along" with the police on the manhunt for Kramer.

The fourth reporter, Sally Everly, a friend of Sammie's, hovered in the visiting area at Massachusetts General Hospital, trying to get in to see her, though she was still recovering from surgery. Sally almost made it past the policeman guarding Sammie's room, using the old flowers-for-the-patient-coffee-for-the-cop trick. It didn't work, but she was able to grab Bob as he came out to take a break from his vigil at her side.

"How's she doing?" Sally asked.

"Great, she's doing great," said Bob. But his face told another story. Pale, drained, with purple bruises under his eyes, he went on, "She's awake, and she wants to see the kids. She's in pain, but not too horrible." He added that she had been talking to the police and thought she knew who did it. "Mostly," he added, "she just wants to get back to work. The nurses are having a hard time keeping her quiet."

"Want to sit down for a minute?" Sally touched Bob's arm gently and led him to the waiting room.

"Yeah, but I might fall asleep if I do." Through his weariness, he no longer knew what time it was.

Bob settled himself on the soft, worn armchair and got out his phone to call Liam and Beau. Sammie's parents were still at the house, too, so Bob talked to all four of them, one at a time. Finally, he leaned back for a minute and rested his head on the back of the armchair. Within minutes, the waiting room was filled with the sound of his gentle snoring.

KRAMER HAD SPENT Sunday night hiding out in a toolshed in a neighbor's garden near his Brookline home, managing three or four hours of sleep. He awoke early, as the newspapers were being delivered—the Monday *Times* landing on doorsteps up and down the block. Seeing multiple police and other unmarked cars outside his house, he debated whether to sneak behind the bushes to his neighbor's front door and snatch the paper. He decided against it, figuring he'd buy a paper later, somewhere farther from his house.

He climbed on his bike and warily biked backstreets to a Dunkin' Donuts. He bought a copy of the *Times* from a newsstand outside, tucked it under his arm, and went inside. The two servers behind the counter, conversing in animated Spanish, barely looked up as they gave him his coffee and muffin. He sat at a small table and read Sammie's follow-up to her Sunday story, then gasped when he read the story about the attack on her.

He downed the rest of his breakfast hurriedly, then went to the men's room. Inside a stall, he took off his fleece jacket and dug his white "doctor" coat and stethoscope out of his backpack. He put them on, took a ratty white handkerchief out of his pants pocket, and stuffed it in the coat pocket so that his once-illustrious name, Dr. Saul Kramer, embroidered in red on the pocket didn't show. He put on his sunglasses and assessed the beginnings of a salt-and-pepper beard. He hadn't shaved in several days. Good. He could barely recognize himself.

The servers behind the counter, a little busier now, didn't look up as he walked out and climbed on his bike. He rode quickly to Newton Centre, locked his bike and helmet in the bike rack, and climbed on the Green Line train to Park Street in downtown Boston. He changed to the Red Line for the quick ride to Charles Street. To his relief, the trains by now were full of early commuters, none of whom seemed interested in just another doctor heading toward Mass General.

Against his better judgment, he was obsessed with finding Sammie. He just had to see her, especially after this morning's news that she had been attacked in the *Times* parking lot. With an arrow, no less.

He felt, what, exactly? He was lousy at introspection, as Ellen had often told him, but there was a feeling lurking just below his consciousness. Jealousy, that's what it was. For some reason, he had a rival out there. Someone else who wanted her dead. But who? And why? After all, he, of all people, had the most reason to kill her. Didn't he? His mind flashed briefly on a story he had read a while ago by Samantha Fuller. That hatchet job from the *Lowell Daily* that the *Times* had picked up. Something about a night editor—Green, was it?—trying to rape her in an elevator. Too bad she'd gotten away. That guy might really be out for blood.

On the other hand, was there someone out there taking his side? Some grateful parent who had managed to have a child because of him? Or one of the younger scientists from his lab fearful of the lab being shut down, and his or her career with it? Or just some random crazy who believed the press was the enemy of the people?

He strode into Mass General. He took no note of the disheveled man walking past him back toward the parking garage.

24

JULY 2019

Ricardo and Heather kept trying the *Times*, repeatedly being told that Samantha Fuller was out and that they could leave a message. No, the scientists kept telling reception, this was urgent. They didn't want to leave a message.

Exasperated, Ricardo glanced down at the morning paper and froze when he read the story on the crossbow attack. Of course Samantha Fuller wasn't in the newsroom. She was in the hospital. The story had been written by the editor himself. Ricardo called again, begging the operators to put him through to Jake Gordon. This time, they did.

"Mr. Gordon," Ricardo began, putting his cell on speaker so Heather could hear. "We are colleagues of Dr. Saul Kramer at the clinic. We'd like to talk."

THAT EVENING SAMMIE settled gingerly on the couch at home, her injured leg propped carefully on a pillow. She had no idea, of course, that Kramer had tried to get in to see her at the hospital and had somehow escaped being recognized, despite the fact that his picture had been in the paper. She didn't know, either, that Joe Green had also tried to see her. From her hospital bed, she had given her story to the police and had talked, and cried, with Bob, but mostly, she had been in and out of consciousness. Now, though, she was alert, tired, but thrilled to be home with her boys and Bob and eager to get back to work.

Liam brought her chamomile tea, Beau brought cookies. Bob was in the kitchen, juggling calls from well-wishers. One plainclothes cop stood guard at the back door and another at the front, both trying unsuccessfully to be inconspicuous.

"The IVF group will be here soon," Bob called from the kitchen. "They're bringing pizza, ice cream, Iggy's bread, and God knows what else."

Sammie smiled her thanks and swallowed another Aleve with a large sip of wine, which was way better than chamomile tea. She gave each of her boys a long hug, cuddling them as best she could without letting them get too close to her wounded leg. It hurt like hell, but she had insisted on getting off the heavy drugs as soon as possible.

"Did you really get shot with an arrow?" asked Beau, trying to sound more worried than impressed."

"I did," Sammie answered. "The doctors took the arrow out of my leg and gave it to the police to look for fingerprints."

"Wow," said Liam. "So they can find the guy who did it?"

"That's the idea," she said.

"Can I have the arrow when the cops are done with it?" Beau asked.

Sammie laughed and ruffled his hair. It was clear he hadn't had a shampoo recently. "Maybe, lovey, maybe."

"Do you know who did it?" Liam asked. Sammie caught Bob's warning glance.

"I think so," she said. "I think it was somebody who didn't like something I wrote in the paper."

"The bad doctor who killed those babies?"

"No, I don't think so," she said. "I think it was someone else." She didn't think a crossbow was Kramer's style.

"Sam, the ladies are here, and they're hungry," Bob called as he answered the door.

Chattering noisily, the women poured in, arms full of food and flowers. They put the food down on the dining room table, then swarmed into the living room, a tsunami of motherly energy, taking turns hugging her, Bob, and the boys. Their contagious energy filled the room, everybody talking at once, people tripping over each other to bring her food. They kept the mood light, joking, lying to her about how great she looked. But their faces were lined with worry.

The boys stayed close to her, soaking in the adult talk, trying to catch enough to understand what had really happened. Bob hovered, too, refilling wineglasses, handing out napkins and keeping an eye on the clock. These women were the best medicine for her, he knew, but Sammie also needed rest.

After a while, a quiet calm descended on the group. Josie scooted over to sit next to Sammie and spoke softly. Her face had matured. Grief over losing little Jamie had softened her features, etching a permanent sadness into her mouth and eyes. But there was a new wisdom there, too, side by side with deep anger.

"My practice seems to be changing," she told her. "Yesterday, those women who contacted you on Sunday when your story ran called me." She said the women wanted to become her patients and she had agreed to treat them, free.

Eventually, Bob raised his eyebrows to signal Liam and Beau that it was time for bed. Tired, they said their goodnights, kissed Sammie, and went off without a fuss for tooth-brushing.

"It's almost your bedtime, too, Sam," he said, looking around at this group of women who, he knew, had become almost as important to her as family. The women got the message, taking dirty dishes to the kitchen and wrapping up leftovers for Bob and Sammie and the kids. One by one, they kissed her good night. After they left, the room felt changed, still vibrating with the women's love, still echoing the precious interconnectedness of their lives.

JOE GREEN WAS furious. He'd tried to get into the post-surgery floor at Mass General but had been blocked by a cop standing guard. The encounter had been brief.

"No visitors. None. Nobody. Sorry," added the officer, who wasn't.

Pissed, Green had driven back to the Lowell trailer camp, stopping at a convenience store on the way to load up with more nachos, beer, and beef jerky. That night, on his second beer, he heard someone outside his trailer. Funny, he hadn't heard a car pull up. He grabbed his crossbow, inserted an arrow, and cautiously approached the door.

"Who is it? Who's out there?" he growled.

"I need to speak to you," said the mysterious voice. "I tracked you down. I know you shot Samantha Fuller."

"Are you the police?" asked Green, still not opening the door.

"No, I'm a doctor."

"What the hell?" Curiosity trumping caution, Green opened the door a crack. "Saul Kramer! I recognize you from your picture in the paper!" Kramer was gaunt and still unshaven, but Green had an editor's eye for faces.

"Correct," said Kramer. "May I come in? I'm unarmed."

Keeping the crossbow on one arm, Green opened the door and nodded for Kramer to sit in his extra chair. "Beer?"

"No, thanks," said Kramer, dropping into the chair. He was sweaty from biking the twenty miles to Lowell.

"You stink," said Green, putting down the crossbow and picking up his beer.

"I rode my bike," said Kramer. He explained that his car was outside his clinic and he obviously couldn't go there. After he had remembered Samantha's story on Green's attempted rape, Kramer had called the city desk at the *Lowell Daily* and posed as an AP reporter doing a follow-up. The intern on the desk had been bored and chatty, telling Kramer that the buzz in the newsroom was that Green had bought himself a trailer and moved to a trailer park outside Lowell. Kramer had thanked the kid and clicked his phone off.

"Shit," said Green. He swigged the last of his beer and got up to go to the tiny fridge to get another. "So, why? Why did you come here?"

"I'm asking the questions," said Kramer. "I need to know one thing. Two, actually."

"What?" asked Green.

"Why did you try to kill Samantha Fuller?"

"Because she wrote about me in the paper. Said I abused her, attacked her in the elevator at the paper, her old paper. Mine, too. Here, in Lowell."

"Did you? Did you attack her?"

"Fuckin' right I did. She deserved it, coming on to me all the time. Wearing those short skirts, teasing me. She ratted me out later, front-page story in the *Daily*."

Kramer was silent for a moment.

"She ratted me out, too. Front page of the *Times*."

"For killing those babies," Green nodded. "I saw the story."

"Yeah, so? Their parents were Nazis, or could have been."

"So, what do you want me for?"

"What do you think?"

Green stared at his beer silently for a moment, then looked up. He got it.

"How much?"

"Fifty."

"Fifty grand?" Green raised his eyebrows so high they almost touched his hairline.

Kramer took a huge wad of hundreds out of his backpack and handed them to Green. A down payment.

"Don't wait too long," he added, getting up. "She'll keep writing until we stop her."

Green held the door open for Kramer to leave. As Kramer pedaled off, his bike light piercing the darkness ahead of him, Green watched, then spat hard on the steps Kramer had just gone down.

"Stupid fucker."

25

JULY 2019

Bob dropped Sammie off at the *Times* the next morning. When she hobbled into the newsroom on crutches, her leg still dramatically bandaged, several reporters stood up from their desks and walked quickly over to her, congratulating her on her Kramer stories and asking about her leg.

Leaning on one crutch, she shook hands with one reporter after another, slowly making her way to her desk. Even Jake Gordon strolled over, high-fiving her as she sat down at her desk.

"Great to see you, Sammie," he said, beaming. "We've got another humdinger for tomorrow. Come on into my office when you're ready. I'll carry your laptop."

Sammie greeted a few more friends, then crutched over to Gordon's office, settling into an extra desk there. Gordon escorted Ricardo Caney and Heather Dungan in along with two others and introduced Sammie to the lawyers they had hired. Sammie had no problem with the lawyers being there, as long as they kept their mouths shut.

"You've met Ricardo and Heather at the clinic, I understand," Gordon began. "They can corroborate everything you wrote. And more."

"Great," Sammie said, opening her laptop. "We're on the record, right? And Jake, we're recording?"

"Yes," he nodded first to Ricardo and Heather, then to her. "I've got our lawyers on call to vet everything around four o'clock, assuming your story is done by then."

"It will be," Sammie said, with more energy than she actually felt.

Taking turns and interrupting each other often, Ricardo and Heather recounted how Kramer had seduced them into cooperating on Niemann-Pick research. They finished each other's sentences, talking over each other in their eagerness to flesh out the story.

They looked worn, and no wonder. Their careers were in tatters, at least for the moment. They had aided and abetted their monster boss, albeit unwittingly, but they had been there all along. They could have, probably should have, suspected something, especially after Heather had discovered the dwindling supplies of the mutant Niemann-Pick gene in the fridge, plus the bottles with that strange MSH2 gene, and after Ricardo had surprised Kramer that night in the lab.

They told how Kramer had made them think he was working on a cure, how they had believed him, and how guilty they now felt. Their lawyers scribbled like mad but didn't interrupt, to Sammie's great relief.

Heather lit up when she recounted how she had noticed that the supply of deadly Niemann-Pick genes dropped every once in a while, but then was quickly refilled.

"Remember, Ricardo?" she turned to him. "I was looking in the fridge and I knew there had been twenty mutant genes in there and suddenly there were only fifteen. I counted over and over."

"Yeah, you tapped me on the shoulder and we went off to talk about it right away," Ricardo nodded. Initially, they had had no idea what those other bottles were, either, the ones with that MSH2 gene. They had looked it up, but still couldn't figure out what was happening. He looked at his lawyer for support. "I guess we should have done something right then."

"But what, exactly?" asked Heather, glancing at her own lawyer.

Ricardo sighed, then sat forward to describe the night he went back to get his cell phone and found Kramer alone in the lab, acting weird and defensive.

"Kramer looked like a caged animal that night," said Ricardo. "He looked terrified. He barked at me, really nervous." The lab had been a mess, too, as if Kramer had been moving things around in a frenzy. "I got out of there as fast as I could."

Heather added that Manuel, the janitor, could vouch for the fact that Kramer had spent many a late night alone in the lab. She was sure Kramer's wife could verify that, too.

They acknowledged that they had not directly witnessed Kramer tampering with the embryos, but explained that there was one key step in the IVF process—the preimplantation genetic screening—when Kramer had always worked alone. There was no need for anyone else to be there during that process, they said, adding that working alone for the screening phase had been Kramer's practice for years.

"Circumstantial," Sammie muttered. "We still need more."

She handed Ricardo and Heather the copious notes Bob and Ashlyn had made in their genetic analysis of the deceased babies, the parents of those babies, and the other parents whose babies were healthy.

"Looks like they did all the right tests," murmured Heather, skimming, Ricardo looking over her shoulder. They traded the papers back and forth almost subconsciously, a habit they had formed over years of working together.

"And here are the autopsies of the Steinberg and the Northrup babies," Sammie added, handing them the report.

"Jesus, this is definitely Niemann-Pick," said Ricardo, the fury in his voice competing with the tears in his eyes.

"So, just to be clear," interrupted Sammie. "What killed these babies was Niemann-Pick, not this other gene, this MSH2, right? That was just a red herring. Kramer just threw that in to throw people off the track?"

"Right," said Ricardo and Heather in unison.

Finally, Sammie asked the question on all of their minds: "Do either of you know why Kramer would do this?"

"No, but he was obsessed with Niemann-Pick," mused Heather softly. "He had a baby boy who died of it."

"Yeah, but why would he have put that gene only into some embryos and not others?" Sammie asked.

Nobody knew.

"Did we give you enough to go on?" Ricardo finally asked. "We're obviously in deep shit for our inadvertent roles in this, but we are solidly with you. We want to validate your story and nail this guy."

"Thanks so much to you both. It's a great start," Sammie said, meaning it and thanking them again for their bravery in coming forward.

"I wish we'd been brave enough to catch him in the first place," Ricardo muttered on his way out.

THE NORFOLK COUNTY District Attorney's office was abuzz the next morning thanks to Sammie's front-page story based on the material Ricardo and Heather had given her.

"It's still circumstantial," grumbled one lawyer to the others hunkered over their coffee in the staff room. "It's a newspaper story. Legally, it's still hearsay."

"Not for much longer," said the DA, Paula Vasquez, a woman in her sixties, graying hair cut stylishly short, high heels clicking on the hardwood floor, joining the group and helping herself to coffee. She settled in her chair and crossed her legs, sheathed in her slim purple pantsuit.

Within an hour, the DA's office had called Ricardo and Heather and their lawyers in, offering testimonial immunity in exchange for their information on Kramer. The assistant DA got a copy of the autopsies. And they began the process of subpoenaing Bob Brightman for his testimony as well as his records on the genetic research he and Ashlyn had done on the babies.

By the end of the day, Vasquez's team had enough evidence to go to a judge for search warrants for Kramer's house and the clinic. They already had a copy of the warrant for the arrest of Dr. Saul Kramer on three counts of homicide—Jamie

Northrup, Katy Wilson, and Henry Steinberg. So far, they had no way of knowing how many more babies Kramer might have killed.

KRAMER HADN'T SLEPT much in the shed. He knew the cops, and that damned Samantha woman, too, would talk to Ricardo and Heather soon, if they hadn't already. Ricardo and Heather hadn't actually *seen* him inserting the Niemann-Pick gene into the embryos, the fertilized eggs—he had made sure of that—but he knew they could easily put the pieces together.

He hadn't eaten much, either. He hoped that he could trust Joe Green, that he hadn't promised the strange man fifty thousand dollars for nothing. Then again, Green was in enough trouble himself that Kramer didn't think he would go to the cops to rat him out, though he couldn't know that for sure.

His mind was turning on him. One minute, he felt his usual, blustery self, the next, panic set in. He wondered about Ellen. His kids? He had never known whether they loved him. Had he ever loved them? He decided to leave the shed. Before he left, he grabbed a small hand shovel that was leaning against the wall. He put it in his backpack and noticed semiconsciously that the handle stuck out a little.

He also grabbed a hammer and smashed his cell phone to bits. He would dump most of the pieces in a series of trash bins he passed on his bike.

He unlocked his bike, fastened his helmet, and took off.

He pedaled one more time to a branch of his bank, one where he was sure nobody knew him. He wore his Red Sox cap with the brim down low and hid his eyes behind his sunglasses. He was counting on the idea that the young, bored-looking teller whose window he picked would not recognize his name or face from the *Times* story.

He had been withdrawing large sums since he realized the *Times* was working on a story on him. Today, he stood under a large maple outside the bank and stuffed $25,000, in hundreds, into a manila envelope. It wasn't the full $50,000 he had promised Joe Green, but if the asshole really came through with the deal, he'd find a way to get him the rest.

Or not.

Kramer pedaled slowly, unsure of where to go. He could ride to their summer house in Provincetown, at the far tip of Cape Cod, but that was a good hundred miles away and although he had managed the twenty-mile round-trip ride to Lowell, he was in no shape to ride to Ptown. Besides, Ellen might have gone there to get away from him. He couldn't blame her if she had. The kids might go there too. Provincetown was out.

By now, he figured, the cops probably had an all-points bulletin out for him. He congratulated himself silently for not taking his car. He had also been careful not to hail an Uber or Lyft, lest a trace was on his credit card or a driver recognize him from his picture. Surely, he reassured himself, the cops wouldn't be looking for a paunchy old guy on a bike.

But where to go? He didn't dare stay in the shed any longer. That left only one place, a short ride.

His mother.

He knew he was taking a chance. With a warrant out for his arrest, his mother's house might be watched.

Nervous, he rode to a spot around the corner from her Brookline condo. He got off the bike and pretended to be fiddling with the gears. Cautiously, he craned his head to see the condo. No obvious cops or cop cars, and no unmarked cars parked in front thanks to the No Parking zone the town had designated.

He rode to the building and locked his bike and helmet in the sheltered bike area in back. With the hand shovel, he dug a shallow hole near the fifth rosebush from the garden path, placed the manila envelope with $25,000 in cash in the hole, and covered it thoroughly with mulch.

He then shouldered his pack and took the elevator up to her door. JAN SCHWARTZ KRAMER read the bronze plaque outside her door. He rang the bell.

"I've been expecting you," his mother said, unsmiling. "Come in, Saul."

She gathered her bathrobe more tightly around her and shuffled, her feet in old, worn slippers, back to her chair in front of the TV. This morning's *Times* lay scattered on the floor, her coffee cup empty, a brown ring long since etched into the bottom.

Saul put down his pack and shed his jacket.

"Ma?" he began, his voice tremulous like that of a two-year-old caught stealing cookies, not the baritone of a domineering physician. "I . . ."

"I know, Saul. And I know why."

"Isaiah, Great-Grandmother Sarah, Theresienstadt," Saul stopped for a moment. "I had to."

"No, Saul. You didn't."

They stared at each other for an uncertain moment. He had half-hoped that she would be proud of him, because of Sarah and all. Obviously, she wasn't.

"I'm hungry," he said suddenly.

His mother walked with great effort to the kitchen, tears streaming down her face. She took out the rye bread, the cheese, the tomatoes. She dropped butter in the frying pan for a melted cheese sandwich, Saul's favorite. She mopped her eyes with her apron, continuing methodically at the stove, wondering what had happened to her son to make him what he was, then flipped the sandwich over to brown the other side.

She put the hot sandwich, cheese oozing out between the slices of bread, onto a plate and placed it on a place mat in front of Saul.

He hunched over his lunch, elbows on the table, cheese smearing his face, his mouth making little smacking noises. "Do you have any chocolate milk, Ma?" The regression was now complete. It was as if her eight-year-old had just come in from an afternoon of playtime with the neighbors.

"Just skim," she said, pouring him a glass.

His stomach full for the first time in days, Saul leaned back in the kitchen chair, tipping it precariously on its back legs.

"Saul!"

"Sorry, Ma." He eased the chair back down. "Can I take a nap in the spare room?"

"I made up the bed for you," she said, picking up his plate to wash.

Saul slept for three hours. While he slept, she riffled through his clothes and backpack and found his pills. She would dole out the Klonopin and maybe the Xanax to him carefully, cutting down the doses bit by bit. He would yell and cry, but she could stand that. They both knew she was in charge now.

She did not sleep. There was no one she could call. Maybe the rabbi, but that would put him in the same dilemma she was in. Saul was her baby, her only son. A doctor. A Harvard doctor. He had been such a good boy and had grown up to be a good doctor. He helped so many couples have babies. She saw in her mind's eye all the pictures of happy parents and babies wallpapering his office walls.

And how bad was he, really, in the grand scheme of things? Very bad, of course. But she, too, knew how soul-crushing the desperation for revenge could be. They hadn't spoken of Nazis in years, but she knew his heart. A mother knows these things.

Later that afternoon, Saul came out to the living room rubbing his eyes. He stood in front of his mother, who sat rock still in her chair.

"Can I take a shower?" he asked.

She nodded.

"I don't have any clothes."

She, of course, had thought of that. She had been planning his return home since the morning when she read that *Times* story. "Look in the top drawer in your room," she told him. She had stocked it with underwear, socks, two pairs of baggy, old-man jeans, and a couple of long-sleeved, button-down white shirts. Nothing fancy, but her son, her only son, would at least be fed and clean before whatever was to happen next.

For the next two days, mother and son passed the time in the same numb routine. She fed him; he ate. By tacit agreement, they turned off the TV since the story of dead IVF babies had gone national by now. Saul slept fifteen hours a day. His mother, barely at all.

In his "spare" time, Kramer prowled the web, looking for a defense lawyer to take his case. He found one: Eileen O'Connor. She was ridiculously young, but she had sounded strong on the phone and, for whatever reason, probably fame, had agreed to take his case.

On the third day, as Saul was in his room dressing after his shower, his mother quietly picked up the kitchen phone, spoke softly, then hung up. She knew what had to be done. She straightened her dress and changed from her slippers to her shoes.

She went back to the stove, took the pancakes out of the pan, and stacked them on his plate. He sat down as she poured his coffee. He didn't notice her hand trembling or hear the cup rattling on the saucer. Suddenly, a rustle at the door. They both looked up. She hit the buzzer.

Jan Schwartz Kramer's eyes flooded with tears, but her voice was strong. "I love you, Saul. I always will."

Kramer sprang up and lunged furiously at his mother, as three beefy police officers rushed in, tripping over each other in their haste to tackle Kramer. They shoved him onto the floor, cuffing his hands behind his back. His mother turned her back. She couldn't bear the pain of watching it happen.

"Ma! Don't leave me!" Kramer's rage quickly turned to sobs. The cops stared stony-faced, then the Irish cop with the soft blue eyes turned to her sympathetically. She turned to face him.

"Is there anyone we can call for you, Mrs. Kramer?"

"My other child will come as soon as I call her," she answered, tears flowing unstoppable down her face, arms twitching of their own accord, reaching out to try to touch her son one last time.

The officers wrestled the sobbing Kramer to his feet and shoved him roughly to the door. He turned to look at his mother. Their eyes met. He saw her lips moving. He strained to hear.

"I thought leaving your Great-Grandmother Sarah alone in the train station was the hardest thing I would ever do," she was saying quietly.

"But I was wrong. This is."

26

OCTOBER 2019

Josie and Peter decided to try for a baby the old-fashioned way for a few months and then, if necessary, they would do one round of IVF. Period. To her surprise, Josie felt relieved not to start with all the blood tests, scans, and hormone injections just yet. After all they'd been through, a few months of regular sex and wine with dinner was very appealing. Mostly, she wanted to get her marriage back on track. She had missed her husband.

To her relief, her practice was booming again. One evening a week she ran a therapy group for the nine other IVF couples whose embryos Kramer had tampered with and whose babies had died. The couples were relieved to be able to talk about their grief.

Peter attended the sessions, too, and, while everybody agreed to confidentiality, all had said yes when he had asked to tape the meetings. They also agreed to at least consider going forward with a civil suit at some point in the future. Peter stressed that this was not a legal commitment and that nobody's comments would be used in any way without written consent.

The sessions were intense. Tears were plentiful, as were hugs before the goodbyes. Josie made sure that everybody who wanted to had a chance to speak. At almost every session, at least one person, often, but not always, a father, sat silent, head bowed.

"Would you like to speak?" she would ask gently.

Often, the man in question would just shake his head. Other times, the man would look up briefly and say something like, "I can't tonight." Whoever was sitting next to him would put an arm around his shoulder or a hand on his forearm.

SAMMIE HAD HEALED quickly. The antibiotics had staved off infection and within ten days, she had been walking without crutches. Her boys had taken no small pride in looking at the arrow wound on her leg, touching it gently every now and then to be sure it didn't hurt her too much.

But the progress ended there. The police had not been able to get fingerprints off the arrow. Whoever shot it must have worn gloves.

And whoever had shot it might try again. That thought still kept Bob and Sammie awake for hours every night. If she had suspected the archer had been Saul Kramer, she could have rested easy. He was in jail now and unlikely to get out any time soon. But she suspected a more likely possibility: Joe Green. She and Bob had tried to get a restraining order against him, but it was denied for insufficient evidence.

Jake Gordon, thankfully, had been paying for a bodyguard for her for months now. And the *Times* had drastically increased its own security, producing no small amount of grumbling from reporters who now had to show identity badges every time they entered the building. Gordon also paid for off-duty cops to guard her house day and night, with another officer dispatched to escort the kids to and from school.

Despite her anxieties, Sammie had hammered away at her story. A total of nine couples had called or emailed with their own horror stories from Kramer's clinic. She wrote their stories, two or three at a time. The *Times* began running a box on Page One listing the names of the deceased babies as the tally rose.

The state department of public health and the attorney general, as she reported, were looking into the clinic's license and practices. The clinic had been temporarily shut down, prompting a string of stories about what would be done with the embryos still there, in frozen limbo. Among the most poignant stories were those of women who had dragged themselves through the whole IVF process expecting their embryos to be implanted imminently and were now frantic, and furious, petrified that their own precious embryos had been tampered with.

The DA had convened a grand jury and requested that Sammie testify. The lawyer for the *Times* refused, arguing that there were other witnesses, namely Ricardo Caney and Heather Dungan, who could testify.

And testify they did. Because of their cooperation, the DA opted not to charge either of them as accomplices. She also ordered them to return to the clinic, under constant police escort, to examine all the frozen embryos to figure out, if they could, which embryos contained the inserted lethal Niemann-Pick gene. Those embryos would be presented in court as evidence, and the other, untampered embryos could be implanted in the waiting IVF patients.

Finally, DA Paula Vasquez felt she had enough evidence and was more than eager to return Sammie's late-afternoon phone call. Practically bouncing in her chair, Sammie wrote the story for which she had been waiting. She hit the SEND button with a flourish followed by a fist pump.

"IVF Doctor Indicted" screamed the headline the next morning. The arraignment, this time in Superior Court, was quick. Once again, bail was denied, and a court date was set for January 2020. Kramer's mother did not visit him, nor did his children, or his wife Ellen. He festered behind bars, his health deteriorating.

Eileen O'Connor, Kramer's spirited young defense lawyer, had dutifully pled "Not Guilty" for him, but didn't bother to request a change of venue. No court in the country would have been any better for Kramer. He had been vilified everywhere.

"As well he should have been," O'Connor said to herself. "He's a monster. And I'm going to save his ass."

ONCE THE TRIAL date had been set, DA Paula Vasquez had a field day.

"We need poster-sized pictures of each of the deceased babies," she told her staff at the morning meeting on the day of

Sammie's most recent story. She would set up the pictures on easels in the courtroom.

"I'm on it," said her new, eager intern, a twenty-something law student with a sparse beard, oversized glasses, and too much energy. "Everybody's agreed so far."

"How about CRISPR experts to testify?"

"It's going great," said the assistant DA, a young man who eschewed his colleagues' casual attire and made it a point to dress every day as if he would be arguing in court. He read off a list of some of the most impressive names in science, all of whom had vetted Bob Brightman's and Ashlyn Wilson's genetic sleuthing, finding their work rock solid.

"Plus, we've got Ricardo Caney and Heather Dungan," said a third staffer, adding that the two scientists were still busy sorting out which of the stored embryos had been tampered with and keeping meticulous records.

"Ethicists?" Vasquez looked around the room.

"Two folks from the Hastings Center, plus that guy from BU," volunteered the law student. Obviously, he added, Kramer was an unethical shit, but these guys seemed pretty reasonable. And credible. They didn't want to outlaw all human embryo research, but would testify that this was premeditated murder.

"Parents?"

"We've got both Josie and Peter Northrup, and both Suzanne and David Steinberg, very willing to testify. Ashlyn Wilson is willing to fly back from Africa if we need her, though money is a problem," said a fourth staffer.

"We have nine other sets of parents of deceased IVF babies from the clinic," added the fourth staffer. Kramer hadn't been charged with those deaths yet since the state was still investigating, so they wouldn't officially be part of the trial. Several therapists would speak about the emotional suffering the parents had gone through.

"And I've got three pediatricians who can testify to what the babies must have suffered," said a fifth.

Vasquez looked at her notes. She had autopsies, lab notes, and all of Sammie's stories.

And then there was Bob Brightman. Vasquez herself had called Bob in to talk and he had come, a bit disheveled and very quiet. He had been on paid administrative leave from MIT since Sammie's original story ran, and he was clearly showing the stress of being a central figure in the case. He missed his lab, his colleagues, and most of all, his normal peace of mind. He had no doubt that he had done the right thing and was as loyal as ever to Sammie, but he had begun seeing a therapist to deal with his angst over his now-jeopardized future at MIT.

"I don't know if I'll ever get my job back," he lamented to Vasquez during one of their grueling talks in her office. "I don't know if any other lab would even hire me at this point."

He knew that, however noble his motivation, universities can't have their people doing their own research on the side, using university facilities, dragging the university name through the mud.

Vasquez had had nothing much to offer him, except the knowledge that testifying in court would put a serial killer away for life. On their last visit, he had paused at the door, his hand on the doorknob.

"You'd better be right about that," he had said, slowly closing the door.

"Bob's a reluctant witness," Vasquez emphasized to her staff. "We need him." Obviously, since he was married to Samantha Fuller, he wouldn't want to say anything that would undercut anything she'd written. And he was shy, he hated the limelight. "But he's a straight shooter," she concluded. "I think he'll come through. But he's going through hell."

The staffers gathered their notes and coffee cups and high-fived each other.

"We've got this, guys, we're going to nail this asshole," the eager law student said to nobody in particular.

"Just do your homework, kid," cautioned Vasquez. "Passion doesn't win cases. Hard work does."

EILEEN O'CONNOR HAD had to consciously unknot her stomach every time she met with Kramer in prison. He looked worse each time she saw him—his belly was swollen, his face, arms, and legs increasingly skinny. His eyes were sunken, his face pale, yellow, even. For any other client, she might have been able to gin up some sympathy. But for Kramer, there simply was none.

This was not about saving this despicable sod, but about rocketing her career into orbit. She knew it would help her case if he could put on a little weight and exercise a little in the prison yard to get some color in his face, but that was clearly not going to happen. Patiently, she walked him through her questions.

He sat dejectedly in the visiting area of the prison, his legs shackled, his wrists in handcuffs. He slumped in his chair, barely noticing the prison guards who stood watching over him and the other inmates talking to their lawyers.

"Were the fertilized eggs alive when you sent them for implantation?" O'Connor asked the question in her least threatening voice.

"Yes."

"They were viable?"

"Yes."

"Did they all have the full complement of chromosomes?"

"Yes."

"Did all the embryos implant successfully?"

"Yes."

She did not ask what he had done with the fertilized eggs during the preimplantation screening. She did not ask why the babies of some parents died while others in the same group of IVF patients didn't. She did not ask what he thought the deceased babies died of. She did not ask if he or anyone in his family had had, or been carriers of, Niemann-Pick disease. She did not want to know. As long as she didn't ask, and he didn't volunteer, she could more or less truthfully assume he was innocent.

What Kramer didn't know was what else Eileen O'Connor had been working on during all the other hours she was billing him for.

27

The Dedham courthouse was packed, and not just the courthouse. Officials had set up a large TV in a nearby school auditorium for the overflow crowd. The main parking lot was jammed with TV trucks. The adjacent lot was crammed, too.

Dr. Saul Kramer stood bleary-eyed and shaky before the district court judge. His story had riveted the world for six months as the prosecution and defense had readied their cases. His name was a household word, a synonym for evil. As his fame, or infamy, had spread, his body had shrunk. He was gaunt, probably no more than 150 pounds now, down from his normal 210.

Part of him was clinging tenuously to his pride. But inside, he was a ping-pong ball, bouncing back and forth between his old arrogance and his new shame. He had scanned the courtroom and, to his relief, had not spotted his mother there to witness his disgrace.

Kramer looked at his lawyer, practically a teenager. Had this kid really gone to law school and passed the bar? She was younger than his daughter, for God's sake. But she had impressed him on the phone in his mother's apartment when he had first spoken to her, and after that, when she had visited him in his cell. He wasn't sure why she had agreed to take his case. Probably because she had seen a chance to make a name for herself, maybe even on the national stage, given the high-profile nature of the case.

Sammie's front-page story yesterday on the prosecution's opening statement had been dynamite. Everyone waited in anticipation to see how the defense could possibly parry that today.

DA Vasquez looked as fresh and on her game this morning as she had yesterday—high heels, same Armani suit, same determination to find Dr. Saul Kramer guilty of murder for the deaths of Jamie Northrup, Katy Wilson, and Henry Steinberg.

Once the jury had settled into their seats, Eileen O'Connor walked slowly toward them. She wore a simple black suit, with no jewelry. She was the very picture of a hardworking, nononsense attorney. No glamour needed. She knew precisely what she was doing.

"This defense will be upsetting to all of you," she began, nodding first to Kramer, who now sat slumped, his face jaundiced and his shoulders collapsed, and then to the jurors. She had not outlined her defense to Kramer, lest he say anything to prison guards or other prisoners who might then leak it to the outside world.

"There is no doubt that these three innocent children died, and died horrible deaths." She gestured to the larger-than-life portraits on easels across the courtroom. "There is also no doubt, as I will show when the medical experts testify, that all three of these children died of Niemann-Pick disease."

"And there is no doubt," she went on, her voice rising, "that the parents of these children did not carry the genes for Niemann-Pick and that there is no way they could have passed this gene on to their embryos. Our expert witnesses, all experts in genetics and CRISPR, will attest to that."

"But," and here she paused, as the courtroom collectively held its breath in anticipation, "the defense will argue that, despite any actions by my client, despite the horrible deaths of these children, Dr. Saul Kramer is not a murderer."

At the mention of his name, Kramer came abruptly to life, sitting bolt upright. At the same time, from the back row of the courtroom, a male voice erupted: "What the fuck?" Joe Green, clearly furious, was hastily removed from the courtroom by two burly guards. Kramer not a murderer? How could that be? He clearly was, the slimy son of a bitch.

Sammie, too, had startled. She was stunned to see Joe Green and could only imagine one reason for him to be there.

The courtroom came to life, too, forcing the judge to bang his gavel repeatedly.

"Order, order," he said loudly. "The courtroom will come to order." The buzzing in the crowd diminished, but did not disappear.

"Please," said O'Connor, turning away from the jury to hush the courtroom crowd herself. "I'm not finished."

Turning back to the jury, she continued. "You don't have to like Dr. Saul Kramer. You don't have to like what he did. You can even be sickened by it, appalled, outraged. But you cannot convict him of murder for one simple reason: Murder, by definition, involves the killing of a person. And an embryo is not a person. Period."

O'Connor let the sudden silence bolster her case as she walked solemnly back to her seat. The jurors squirmed, wanting, but not daring, to talk to each other. Sammie typed away furiously, as did the rest of the press corps. O'Connor's presentation had been so spellbinding no one realized it had taken most of the morning.

Paula Vasquez rose slowly from her seat.

Vasquez was an ardent, vocal, dues-paying supporter of pro-choice groups across the country, the ACLU, the National Organization for Women, NARAL, Planned Parenthood—all of them.

She had had an abortion years ago, a safe one, thanks to *Roe v. Wade*, and had never once thought of that embryo as a person. She vehemently disagreed with the "personhood" movement the right-to-lifers were pushing. In her gut, she knew O'Connor was right, that an embryo is not a person. But she also knew that legally, that didn't change a thing. Kramer caused those babies' deaths. Period. She hoped the jury could understand that. In her mind's eye, she saw the pictures of the dead babies. Clearly, he was a monster, a killer.

She was just beginning to address the jury when the judge announced a recess. "We will resume this afternoon at one p.m."

Sammie led the dash out of the courtroom, laptop bouncing in its bag against her shoulder, cell phone in hand.

"Jake," Sammie shouted into the phone as she raced toward her car for privacy. "The defense is using the 'embryo-is-not-a-person' argument."

Jake, sounding gruffer than he meant, said, "Just write the thing. Call me when you hit SEND."

Sammie took a protein bar out of her glove compartment and settled herself in the roomier passenger seat of her car to write. A few reporters banged on her window, but she waved them off and mouthed, "Not now."

"In a stunning, surprise move this morning in the CRISPR murder trial of the IVF doctor, Dr. Saul Kramer, defense attorney Eileen . . ." Sammie typed. Her fingers flew. Her brain was on fire.

As she worked, other *Times* reporters deluged the paper's librarians with requests for archived stories on the "personhood" movement being stoked by anti-abortionists. The legal columnist started his piece on the history of *Roe v. Wade* and attempts to overturn it. Other reporters began calling professors at leading law schools across the country.

JOSIE, PETER, AND the Steinbergs, as prosecution witnesses, had not been in the courtroom in the morning, but had sat on benches in the hallway outside. But secrets don't last long in big trials. They heard what happened as the crowd poured out of the courtroom and headed for lunch.

"I can't believe it," fumed Peter, jumping to his feet. "Using the personhood argument. If he gets off on that . . . I can't even think about it." His son was a person. A real-life person whom he loved with all his heart. He realized he was talking to no one in particular, but didn't care.

Josie, seated next to the Steinbergs, tried frantically to text Ashlyn Wilson in Africa, but her tears kept falling onto her cell phone. Suzanne Steinberg reached over and touched her on the arm. Reporters, realizing who this small, emotional group was, started to swarm, wanting to know their reaction to the news of the defense.

"Let's get out of here, the four of us," said Suzanne urgently. "There's a pub down the street."

Gathering purses and briefcases, the four parents, their fresh despair colliding with long-standing grief, walked in shock to the pub. DA Vasquez had beat them there, already huddling with her staff in a corner trying to regroup for the afternoon session.

Vasquez barked to her staff.

"I need somebody to bring me all the stuff on embryo personhood cases, now. It's in our files." They should have brought all that to court. She nodded to the young law student, who grabbed his laptop and rushed out to the office. The rest of the team squeezed closer together, trying, but failing, to keep their voices down. Vasquez looked up for a moment and spotted the four parents just taking their seats at another table. She sighed.

At their own table, the parents stared at their menus as the waitress shifted from foot to foot, tapping her pencil on her notepad.

They ordered three beers and a water. None of them was hungry.

THAT AFTERNOON, JOSIE Reimann Northrup took the witness stand. She tried to sit up straight, telling herself to stay strong for little Jamie. Sammie focused all of her energy on telegraphing strength and courage to her.

Under gentle, painstaking questioning from Paula Vasquez, Josie told her story over the next two hours. The hard decision to do IVF, the ups and downs of the medical tests, the injections, the mood swings. Then the joy of Jamie's birth, the horror at watching her baby die, the agony of her friend Ashlyn's baby's slow, torturous death, then the even greater agony of realizing that their deaths had been no accident.

"Do you consider Dr. Saul Kramer a murderer?" asked Vasquez, standing near Josie and looking at her encouragingly.

"Objection! That is for the jury to decide!" cried Eileen O'Connor, jumping up. But before the judge could rule on the objection, Josie said loudly, looking directly at the jury: "Yes. He killed my son. On purpose. He is a murderer."

The judge called for Josie's response to be struck as he granted the objection and called a fifteen-minute recess. By 3:30, Josie was drained, but congratulated warmly by Vasquez for getting through the direct questioning. She took her seat again, pausing to look at the poster-sized picture of little Jamie on the easel. A moment not lost on the jurors.

Eileen O'Connor tried to be gentle. She felt Josie's anguish and did not want to come off as a cold-blooded defense attorney to the jury, but she had a job to do.

"Do you consider yourself a feminist?" she began.

Josie nodded, sensing where this was going.

"Please speak into the microphone," cautioned the judge.

"Yes, I am a feminist," Josie answered.

"Do you believe in a woman's right to choose whether or not to have an abortion?"

Paula Vasquez jumped to her feet to challenge. "Objection. Relevancy. This case is not about abortion."

"Overruled," said the judge. "Let the defense proceed."

"Please answer the question," said O'Connor.

"Yes, I firmly believe in a woman's right to choose," answered Josie.

"Do you believe a fertilized egg or an embryo is a person?" O'Connor felt her stomach churn as she posed the question. She hated herself for asking, barely able to look at Josie.

Josie did not answer. The clock ticked slowly, the only sound audible in the courtroom. The jurors leaned forward, those in the front row bracing their arms on the railing.

"I know it is difficult to answer these questions," the judge said kindly. "But please, take a deep breath and answer the question."

Josie looked at Kramer, at Vasquez, finally at Eileen O'Connor.

"No, I do not believe a fertilized egg or an embryo is a person. But what Dr. Kramer did to our embryo, an embryo we went through hell to get, caused our baby's death. It took a year, but Dr. Kramer was the cause of my baby's death."

It was nearing four o'clock. The jurors looked shell-shocked. Josie seemed close to collapse.

"Let's stop here for today," said the judge. "We'll resume tomorrow at nine a.m. sharp."

28

JANUARY 2020

For the next ten days, the trial ground on.

Peter Northrup, like his wife, was on the stand for hours, often sobbing his way through the details of Jamie's conception, birth, and death. Despite his suit and clean-shaven face, he looked physically and emotionally broken. And, it was obvious, in the way he spoke, with tears freely running down his face, that he was.

Suzanne and David Steinberg were similarly tortured by direct and cross examination. There was no way for them not to be. They could barely look at the jury as they described their desperate efforts to conceive and their joy in Henry's birth, knowing how the story ended.

To everyone's surprise, Vasquez had managed to fly Ashlyn Wilson back from Africa. It was a bittersweet reunion with the other parents, but as a molecular biologist, Ashlyn's testimony was doubly valuable to the prosecution. Not only did she tell little Katy's story, but she set the tone for Bob Brightman, Ricardo Caney, and Heather Dungan to testify about Kramer's deadly tampering of the embryos.

In an effort to set the stage for Kramer's motive, Vasquez asked Ashlyn what her heritage was, just as she had asked the Steinbergs and the Northrups. And just as both those couples had answered, Ashlyn replied that she had German lineage.

"Did you know that both the Steinbergs and the Northrups have some German in their heritage, just like you?" asked Vasquez.

"I guess that's just one more thing we have in common. That is, in addition to making the fatal mistake of going to Dr. Kramer for help," she replied.

Sammie was excited to see Ashlyn again and to have her expertise buttress the case against Kramer. But DA Vasquez's next witness was a stunner: Kramer's own mother, Jan Schwartz Kramer. The eighty-five-year-old woman did not look at her son as she walked slowly aided by her cane to the witness stand. She stood dignified, solemn, as she was sworn in, still avoiding eye contact. She sat, adjusting her skirt and clasping her hands in her lap.

"Thank you for testifying today," Vasquez began gently. "I know, we all know, how hard this must be for you."

Vasquez then walked Kramer's mother through the story of the family's escape from Vienna and the sorrow of leaving her grandmother in the train station, and her ultimate demise at the hands of the Nazis.

"Do you hate the Nazis?" Vasquez asked.

Mrs. Kramer didn't answer. She looked up to the judge. He nodded and said, "Mrs. Kramer, please answer the question."

"Yes, I do," she answered.

"Does your son, Dr. Saul Kramer, hate the Nazis?"

"Yes, he does," she answered.

"Can you tell us how he learned about the family history and what his reactions were?"

Mrs. Kramer recounted how she had told the story many times to Saul and that no matter how many times he heard it, he would ask her to tell him again. That despite the nightmares he would have every night after they talked about the Nazis, he would have the same request—to hear about them again.

"So, you understand his motivation for killing these babies?" Vasquez moved closer to the witness stand.

"Objection!" screamed Eileen O'Connor, jumping out of her seat at the defense table.

"Sustained. Ms. Vasquez, please rephrase," said the judge, looking sternly at the DA.

Vasquez apologized and continued, "Mrs. Kramer, can you understand why Dr. Kramer would have injected the embryos with the deadly gene?"

The courtroom held its breath. Mrs. Kramer took her time.

"No, I cannot," she said finally. "What he did was wrong. He is no better than the Nazis. I love my son, but I cannot forgive him for what he did." She was careful not to look at him as she spoke, tears welling up in her eyes.

"Is that why you called the police on him?" Vasquez asked.

"Yes. That is why," Mrs. Kramer said, softly.

"No further questions."

Eileen O'Connor stood up to begin her cross. Kramer looked on, his eyes welling up with tears as he silently hoped his attorney would show kindness to his beloved mother.

"Mrs. Kramer," she began, "did you do anything to quell the hatred you saw your son developing for the Nazis?"

"Well, no. I also hate the Nazis for all they took away from me. Lots of people hate the Nazis," Mrs. Kramer countered.

"Agreed," said O'Connor. "And did you think that your son's hatred was anything more than what most of us feel for this despicable group of people?"

"Well, no, I didn't. But that was before—"

O'Connor cut her off. "Thank you. No further questions."

After a short break, testimony resumed. This time, the prosecution witness was Ellen Kramer, Kramer's wife.

Like his mother, Kramer's wife did not look at her now-former husband. Under Vasquez's questioning, she testified that she thought she had loved her husband in the early years of their marriage, though she admitted she had begun to question that recently, along with everything else in their relationship except their children. She had been increasingly puzzled, she admitted, by Kramer's frequent late nights in the lab, even wondering if he had been having an affair. She had also wondered, she said, about the almost-manic energy he had suddenly seemed to have.

Cautiously, Vasquez then asked Ellen to describe how her husband had reacted after their baby son, Isaiah, died. Ellen Kramer had asked for a tissue and a moment to collect herself.

"After Isaiah died," she began, her voice cracking, "we went briefly into bereavement counseling." Saul hated every minute of it, she went on. As a "real" doctor and research scientist—she used her hands to show air quotes—he didn't have much respect for psychiatrists. He called them "weaklings," "babysitters," "hand-holders."

Vasquez stayed silent, letting Ellen Kramer take her time and giving the jury time to digest the so-called real doctor's feelings.

"Our bereavement therapist was actually a well-respected psychiatrist," she went on. "He kept asking Saul about his feelings."

"How did your former husband respond?" Vasquez probed.

"Am I allowed to use his actual words? He swore," asked Ellen Kramer.

"Yes, you may," said Vasquez.

"He said, 'What the fuck do you think my feelings are?' He was enraged. The psychiatrist kept asking if he was sad, too, but Saul just insulted the doctor."

"And then?" asked Vasquez.

"After one session, he kept repeating the word 'failure.' I asked him what he meant." He said he had failed Isaiah and his Great-Grandmother Sarah. He said, "Failure, failure, failure." When she had asked what he meant, he said that failure was what the shrink should have asked about.

O'Connor stood quickly. "Objection. Hearsay."

The judge overruled the objection and turned his attention back to the witness stand.

"What happened then?" continued Vasquez.

"He started keeping his mouth shut after that. We quit therapy, though I kept going alone, myself. But . . ." Ellen Kramer trailed off.

"But what?" asked Vasquez.

"Saul told me one night after he had had a couple of drinks—he didn't drink much usually—that he would sometimes sit for hours outside the German consulate in Boston watching people go in and out, guessing which ones might be Nazi sympathizers."

"He also told me that, after I was asleep at night, he would prowl pro-Nazi websites trying to figure out who was in charge and whether he could kill the leaders."

"And what did you say when he told you this?"

"I didn't say much. I didn't know what to say."

Vasquez let that sink in for a moment, then asked Ellen Kramer if, looking back, there were any other clues about her husband's mental state or activities.

"I looked in his briefcase once after he told me these things, and I saw bottles of Klonopin, Xanax, and Ambien with my name on them."

"Were those pills you took regularly?"

"No. He must have prescribed them without my knowing, so he could take them himself."

O'Connor jumped up. "Objection! Speculation."

"I'll allow it," said the judge. "But go easy, Ms. Vasquez."

Vasquez asked if Ellen Kramer wanted to take a break. She shook her head. It was obvious in her demeanor that she just wanted to get this over with as quickly as possible.

"Finally, in the last months that you were together, before all this became public, did you notice any change in his mood or behavior?"

"Yes," said Ellen Kramer, "though I didn't make sense of it at the time. He spent many nights in the lab." Sometimes, she said, he didn't come home for dinner at all. She thought he was making great progress on his research, and when she asked him, he said he was.

"And his mood at these times?" asked Vasquez.

"He was happy."

"No further questions."

Eileen O'Connor stood up and walked over to the witness stand.

"Mrs. Kramer, wasn't your husband a brilliant doctor?"

Ellen Kramer hesitated. "I thought so."

"Well, didn't he help thousands of couples over the years have babies they never would have been able to have otherwise?"

"Yes, he did."

"And, in all that time, he never had any complaints against him?"

"As far as I know, no. But . . ."

"That is all," O'Connor said quickly.

AFTER A LUNCH break, Vasquez resumed her case.

She called three independent expert witnesses, all CRISPR researchers. One by one, she peppered them with questions. She took her time guiding the jurors through the intricate details of CRISPR, asking the witnesses to break it down as much as possible into layman's terms. She used diagrams on posters and PowerPoint slides, going over the basics of the science, and then going over it again.

All three CRISPR witnesses explained how Kramer could have easily, although not ethically, done what he did. All three corroborated what Ashlyn Wilson and Bob Brightman had discovered months ago—that none of the three deceased babies had parents who carried the Niemann-Pick gene, and as such that gene had to have been inserted artificially.

Witness by witness, Sammie could see the subtle changes on the jurors' faces. They were getting it, God bless them. She could barely restrain herself from giving Vasquez a thumbs-up.

And at the end of the examination of each CRISPR expert, Vasquez asked the essential question.

"In your expert opinion, if Dr. Kramer had not tampered with the embryos, the fertilized eggs, do you believe those babies would be alive today?"

"Yes, they would," said the first expert.

The second expert answered the same.

The third CRISPR expert was a woman, four months pregnant. Vasquez steeled herself to be heartless.

"I see that you are pregnant, correct?" Vasquez asked.

"Yes, I am pregnant."

"And do you feel that you are carrying a baby, a person? Or an embryo? Or a fetus?" Vasquez pressed the point.

"I am a scientist," said the witness, fighting tears. "I am also a mother-to-be." She patted her baby bump. "Technically, I am carrying a fetus. It started out as a fertilized egg, then an embryo, which implanted into my womb. It will become a baby, a person, when it is born."

"Do you think anyone will give you a shower?"

"Yes, my friends and my mother and my husband's mother."

"They won't call it a 'fetus shower' or an 'embryo shower,' will they?" Vasquez hated herself for asking.

EILEEN O'CONNOR WAS ready. She had only one question for the pregnant witness.

"My question to you is this: Even after being tampered with, were these fertilized eggs, these potential embryos, alive or dead?"

"They were alive," answered the witness.

"Thank you," said O'Connor. "No further questions."

The courtroom buzzed as the pregnant witness stood up, straightened her skirt, and hesitantly walked down from the witness stand, not bothering to hide her tears. The judge banged the gavel once to hush the crowd as the woman took her seat.

Heather Dungan and Ricardo Caney, the prosecution's star witnesses, were next on the prosecution's list. Heather went first. She was eloquent, often stopping to collect herself. She spoke of how they had no idea what was going on until it was too late, how Kramer had tricked them into unknowingly cooperating under the guise of valid, groundbreaking research. She explained that after Kramer's arrest, they had gone back to the lab, under police guard, and found the stored fertilized eggs, including some into which Kramer had inserted the deadly gene. Close-up pictures of those tampered-with eggs were displayed on large easels near the defense table.

When the DA completed her examination, O'Connor began her cross.

"Ms. Dungan, did it ever cross your mind that tampering with fertilized eggs is, at a minimum, unethical?"

Heather hesitated ever so slightly before answering, "No, we are scientists and were trying to help others with our research."

Heather was clearly upset and beginning to get frazzled, her own guilt for not doing more to prevent this tragedy seeping into her words. O'Connor paused.

"Help others? Aren't you now testifying that what Dr. Kramer did was wrong?"

"Yes, but we didn't know at the time what he was doing."

"No further questions for this witness."

RICARDO WAS UP next. He passed Heather on the way to the witness stand, sharing a quick, concerned glance. After he was sworn in, the DA asked him when he had understood the full ramifications of what had happened. He explained that it was the day Sammie's story had run. That was when they truly understood the depths of what had been going on and how they had inadvertently helped Kramer. His emphasis on the word "inadvertently" was not lost on anyone.

Vasquez then asked the bailiff to dim the courtroom lights, explaining that she would be playing a video. The dimmed lights cast a surreal glow in the courtroom as her assistants set up a projection screen and projector.

"What I am about to show you is footage the state has obtained from the security cameras in Dr. Saul Kramer's lab." She noted that there were, as one would assume, many hours of footage of Dr. Kramer alone at night in his lab. She was only going to show the jury a few critical moments. The audio was faint, she added, asking everyone to listen carefully and remain as silent as possible so that everyone could hear.

Her assistant flicked on the projector. The courtroom was deathly still. The screen lit up, showing Ricardo Caney approaching the door to the Kramer lab.

Vasquez pressed PAUSE on the remote control she picked up from her table. "Mr. Caney, is that you in the video?"

"Yes, it is."

"Is that the entrance to the Kramer lab?"

"Yes."

She pressed Play again.

"*Saul!*" Ricardo's voice echoed through the courtroom.

"*What the fuck? What the hell are you doing here?*" Kramer had not spoken once during the trial, but there was no question whose voice it was. The footage showed him spinning around in his chair to face the intruder.

"*I forgot my cell phone. What are YOU doing here?*"

"*Working. What does it look like?*"

"*I didn't know you were working at night. You work so hard during the day. Don't you need a break?*"

The jurors, visitors, and journalists sat riveted to the screen. Sammie stopped typing. Everyone could see Kramer in the video forcing his shoulders down. They watched him lean back in his chair and arrange his face to appear calmer. They watched him clasp his shaking hands together.

"*I like the peace and quiet.*"

"*Well, don't stay too late,*" Ricardo said after a long pause, "*you need sleep like the rest of us mortals.*"

There was a break in the film at this point, then the spliced footage resumed, showing Ricardo on his way out the door, where he encountered Manuel, the janitor.

"*Manuel,*" Ricardo's voice again filled the courtroom. "*Dr. Kramer, does he come here often at night?*"

"*Sí, sí.*" Everyone could see Manuel nod emphatically. "*Muchas noches.*"

The courtroom fell silent as the prosecution team scurried to set up the next sequence. Vasquez let the silence settle. Anything she said at this point would dilute the impact of what the jurors had just seen. Ricardo shifted uncomfortably on the witness stand. Finally, she spoke up again.

Vasquez nodded to the bailiff to put the lights back on and informed the judge that she had no other questions for Ricardo.

Ms. O'Connor didn't waste any time.

"Why did you go along with it?"

"I didn't know what I was going along with," Ricardo answered defensively.

"Is it possible you were more concerned about your job than those embryos?"

"Absolutely not!"

"Wasn't there talk about a Nobel Prize regarding the work you were doing?"

"Yes, but . . ."

"No further questions," O'Connor interrupted. She had made her point.

The judge, looking drained, turned to Vasquez for her next witness.

The DA stood confidently. "The state rests, Your Honor."

The judge called for a thirty-minute recess. For a few moments, no one moved, then the crowd slowly rose to stretch their legs and use the bathrooms. The court officer escorted the jury out. Sammie raised her eyebrows at Vasquez, the two women trying to hide their growing sense of victory, of a jury vote to convict the monster whom everyone had now seen doing his dark magic.

AFTER THE RECESS, everyone assembled back in the courtroom, moving methodically to their seats. Once they were back in session, Eileen O'Connor stood and called her first witness.

Sammie, along with everyone else, watched as a handsomely graying Harvard law professor took his place on the stand, raising his hand and swearing to tell the truth.

O'Connor faced the jury, introducing the professor, who actually needed no introduction, judging by the nodding heads in the jury box and gallery. His name was a household word thanks to his numerous TV appearances. The constitutional law expert, known partly for his well-reasoned law review articles, but mostly for his controversial defense of unsavory characters, was the picture of dignity as he took his seat. His carefully coiffed gray hair had the enviable shine that could only come from silver-enhancing shampoos and professional blow drying.

Papers in hand, O'Connor began walking the professor through his well-prepared testimony. After a number of questions establishing him as an expert in the law, O'Connor got straight to the point with one poignant question.

Sammie watched, fingers poised on her laptop.

"Have any courts ever ruled that an embryo is legally considered a person?"

"No."

"Thank you," said O'Connor, turning to Paula Vasquez. "Your witness."

PAULA VASQUEZ TOOK her time approaching the law professor. She smiled at him. He did not smile back. Law professor one, DA, zero.

"Professor," she began, obsequious despite herself. "Many states have passed so-called feticide laws, which essentially define a fetus as a person." She paused.

"Is that a question?" asked the professor, not trying to hide a smirk.

"How many states have such laws?" she pressed on.

"To my knowledge, twenty-nine states," he answered, more civilly.

"So, if a fetus can be considered a person, why can't an embryo or a fertilized egg also be considered a person?" She stepped close to him, looking him straight in the eye.

"Objection!" cried O'Connor. "The professor is not testifying about fetuses."

"Objection sustained," gaveled the judge.

Vasquez tried again.

"Professor, if Dr. Saul Kramer tampered with these eggs, these potential embryos, in such a way as to insert a deadly gene intended to kill the baby after it was born, is that not murder?"

O'Connor nearly jumped out of her seat in an instant. "Objection! That is for the jury to decide."

"Sustained. Ms. Vasquez, you know better."

"Nothing further," she said to the judge. Keeping her composure, Vasquez went back to her seat. The corners of her mouth curled up ever so slightly, knowing she got her point across to the jury—objection or not.

"Redirect, Ms. O'Connor?" asked the judge.

"For the record, Professor," said O'Connor, rising to her feet, "what is the legal peril of these feticide laws, and by extension, any law defining an embryo as a fetus?"

"These and other laws allow a pregnant woman to be charged with manslaughter if the state perceives her as recklessly endangering her fetus."

"Thank you, Professor. The defense rests."

Sammie gathered her laptop and raced back to the newsroom.

29

JANUARY 2020

District Attorney Paula Vasquez went first in the closing arguments. Her words, as always, were eloquent. She strode to the jury, consciously straightening her shoulders and lifting her chin. Like everyone else in the crowded courtroom, Sammie listened, mesmerized.

"As you know," she addressed the weary jurors, "the burden of proof is on us, the Commonwealth. And we have met that burden. We have shown beyond a reasonable doubt that Dr. Saul Kramer willfully, with malicious intent, inserted a lethal gene into the embryos that would become Jamie Northrup, Katy Wilson, and Henry Steinberg, causing the death of all three." She barely paused for breath.

Vasquez then began providing the jury instructions to go through the elements of the crime.

"I will begin by instructing you on the elements of murder in the first degree." She explained that the Commonwealth had to prove beyond a reasonable doubt the following: First, that the defendant caused the death of Jamie Northrup, Katy Wilson, and Henry Steinberg. Second, that the defendant consciously and purposefully intended to kill Jamie Northrup, Katy Wilson, and Henry Steinberg. And, finally, that the defendant committed the killing with deliberate premeditation, that is, he decided to kill after a period of reflection.

"We have shown that Dr. Saul Kramer caused the deaths of Jamie Northrup, Katy Wilson, and Henry Steinberg," she said. According to the Commonwealth's jury instructions, she said, "An act is the cause of death where the act, in a natural and continuous sequence, results in death, and without which death would not have occurred." She said that Kramer chose this particular lethal gene consciously, using his extensive knowledge as a geneticist, purposefully intending to kill these babies, satisfying the second element. The third element, she added, was similarly met because his decision was planned over time and a period of reflection. He thought through the entire process. He actually handpicked those who would suffer from his actions.

"He didn't destroy the eggs, the embryos, so whether or not they were legally considered 'persons' at that time is irrelevant," she said. What is relevant, she explained, is that his actions set into motion a sequence of events that caused those three babies to die. That without his actions, those babies would be alive right now. Plain and simple. He played God. Their future lives and deaths rested solely in his hands. His intention and his actions directly caused these babies' deaths. She looked at each juror as she spoke.

"Furthermore, we have learned his motive for these heinous acts: his deep hatred for Nazis due to his own family's experiences in World War II, as his own mother and ex-wife have testified. While this hatred is understandable, it does not justify or excuse his behavior." She reminded the jury that it was his mother, Jan Schwartz Kramer, who had lost her own grandmother to the Nazis and who had turned Dr. Kramer in to the police.

The entire courtroom stirred as people sitting near Kramer's mother, now in the back row, realized she had fainted. Sammie stood up to watch, texted Jake, then sat down again as the judge called a fifteen-minute recess while Kramer's mother was tended to by a nurse who happened to be sitting close by. Sammie took advantage of the break to check her notes and collect her thoughts.

Determined to see the case through, Kramer's mother insisted on returning to her seat, pale and shaky, with an ammonia ampule clutched in her hand. She didn't look at her son, who sat dazed in the defendant's chair, looking jaundiced, bloated, and confused.

O'Connor strode confidently to address the jurors. She waited until she had made lingering eye contact with each one.

"This may be among the most difficult decisions each of you will ever make. I know your hearts go out to Josie and Peter Northrup, to Ashlyn Wilson, to David and Suzanne Steinberg, as well they should.

"The three embryos in this case were clearly tampered with, with evil intent. Of that, there is no question. There is also no question that no one except Dr. Saul Kramer had access to these embryos in moments when he was alone in his lab, that he is the only one who could have done this," she continued.

"But, as horrible as these actions were, Dr. Saul Kramer did not commit murder. Because these embryos, like all embryos, were not 'persons.' Therefore, they cannot be murdered.

"Ms. Vasquez has attempted to persuade you that Dr. Kramer is a murderer. But that attempt cannot be successful because tampering with an embryo, even by inserting an eventually lethal gene, is not murder. Therefore, you must conclude that my client is not guilty."

The judge nodded once more to Vasquez. Because the prosecution has the burden of proof, it gets the last word, a final rebuttal.

Vasquez wasted no time, catching Sammie's eye briefly as she walked slowly over to the jury.

"If it were not for Dr. Saul Kramer's actions, those babies would be alive today. He killed them," she said, tears in her eyes, her voice quaking, yet strong and powerful. "You know that. I know that. Dr. Kramer's mother knows that. Do the right thing. Thank you."

The judge looked sympathetically at the jury.

"Your task in this case is difficult. Please take all the time you need and submit questions to me if you are at an impasse or need clarification. Ultimately, your job is this: to decide whether Dr. Saul Kramer, by inserting a lethal gene into these three embryos, committed murder beyond a reasonable doubt. Court is recessed."

Sammie drove back to the *Times* in a daze. It had all come down to this. The assessment of twelve normal people. Was it murder or wasn't it? Sammie desperately wanted them to find him guilty, after his unspeakable evil and, honestly, after all her own hard work.

And yet, and yet. Sammie, too, believed deeply that an embryo was not a person, that even her own babies had not been persons when they were just embryos. But she also held tightly to Vasquez's argument, that whether the embryos were "persons" or not, that did not change the fact that Kramer caused the babies' deaths. She hoped that the jury could make the distinction.

She sank into her seat at the *Times* and began typing.

AFTER A LONG, front-page story reviewing the prosecution and defense arguments, Sammie thought maybe she could take the next few days off or, at a minimum, function in "low gear." It was not to be. There is no on/off switch for a journalist.

From the minute Sammie walked into the newsroom the next morning, she was glued to her phone. She called lawyers around the country who were not involved in the case for their assumptions about the verdict. She did a quick person-on-the-street story, interviewing people in a shopping mall and on sidewalks to gauge public opinion on the likely outcome. She even fielded calls from half a dozen publishers dangling tempting advances for an "instant book" on the case.

But she hurriedly put all that aside when she learned of a just-called "do-over" meeting at the National Academy of Sciences, Engineering and Medicine, to reexamine the question of gene-editing of embryos. Sammie figured she had just enough time to fly to Washington to cover the meeting, write it up while waiting at the airport, and fly home in time to be in court when the jury came back with a verdict.

OUTSIDE THE COURTROOM, hatred for Kramer and Eileen O'Connor was palpable and growing every day. Busloads of angry evangelicals and pro-lifers from Arizona, Mississippi, Missouri, Florida, and elsewhere descended on downtown Boston. Their rallies in City Hall Plaza grew larger and louder by the day. "An embryo *is* a person!" they shouted. "Kramer is a murderer!" Rumors abounded that the pro-lifers were infiltrated by white supremacists and gun rights crazies hoping to capitalize on the unrest.

Death threats poured into O'Connor's phone line and email. Police mounted a round-the-clock protection effort for her and her family. She reminded herself that this, or at least some of this, was what she wanted. People definitely knew her name now.

Also pouring into Boston by the busload were abortion rights activists. They came from all over the country. At City Hall Plaza, they screamed at the pro-lifers, "An embryo is *not* a person!"

Jake Gordon sent general assignment reporters and photographers to cover the protests. TV networks kept raising their estimates of crowd sizes, fanning the flames. Talking heads from FOX to MSNBC analyzed the embryo-is-not-a-person defense from their respective points of view.

In the secluded woods near his trailer park outside Lowell, Joe Green was busy, too, practicing with his brand-new gun and silencer, his latest acquisitions. Never having handled a gun before, Green had combed the Internet for tips on firing skills and had joined a gun club to practice on targets.

Surprising himself, he discovered that he was actually getting good at it. The crossbow had been hard to learn, but guns were easy. He uttered a silent prayer: "Thank God for the Second Amendment."

THE JURORS WERE a collective mess. The only thing they agreed on was the election of the foreman. A young black woman, with a husband and two grade-school children, won on the third ballot, beating out two middle-aged white men.

They briefly debated whether to take a straw poll on Kramer's guilt or innocence, but abandoned the idea.

Antipathy for Kramer so dominated the first two days of deliberations that no one even brought up the embryo-as-person issue. All they could do was vent. Finally, the forewoman took firmer control.

"We all agree that Kramer is despicable," she said, with as much calm as she could muster. "But what we have to decide is whether he really caused the death of those babies, who didn't exist at the time of his actions, and if so, whether Kramer is guilty, beyond a reasonable doubt, of murder."

It was torture of the deepest kind, within each juror's heart. It took two and a half more days, many tears, heart palpitations, and written procedural questions to the judge. But by mid-afternoon Friday, the forewoman sent a note to the judge that the jury had reached a verdict.

Sammie, just back from Washington, raced to the courthouse along with the rest of the press corps. Jake Gordon ordered the pressroom to prepare for an extra edition. TV networks began broadcasting breaking news alerts.

Paula Vasquez and Eileen O'Connor slipped in the back door of the courthouse together. They nodded to each other in the elevator like wounded soldiers in the same trench. They didn't say a word, nor did they have to.

The pro-lifers marched en masse to the courthouse, kept at a distance from the entrance by riot police wielding shields, tear gas, and guns. Abortion rights activists flocked there, too, as vehemently, or even more so, than the pro-lifers. The air filled with screams as the two sides tried to outshout each other.

Inside, the courtroom slowly hushed as the jury forewoman rose to address the judge.

30

JANUARY 2020

The judge turned slowly toward the jury, nodding to the forewoman.

"Has the jury reached a verdict?"

"Yes, Your Honor."

In the defendant's chair, Kramer jerked straight up, holding his breath. Paula Vasquez held her breath, too. So did Sammie. And so did Eileen O'Connor, who looked, if anything, worse than her client, visibly thinner since receiving the death threats of this past week.

Josie and Peter sat stiffly and held hands tightly, grabbing Ashlyn Wilson's hand in their grip. Nearby, the Steinbergs tensed, shoulders touching, heads bowed in prayer. Behind them, the faithful IVF mothers linked arms and swayed back and forth slightly as one, each struggling still with grief and gratitude simultaneously. Far back, in the last row, Kramer's mother prayed, though exactly for what, she wasn't sure.

Joe Green, also in the far back, harbored no such mixed feelings. He sat rigid in his carefully chosen seat on the center aisle poised for a quick getaway, like a hunting dog ready to pounce. Kramer had promised him $50,000 to kill Sammie. But when, as instructed, he'd gone to dig up the money outside Kramer's mother's condo, there was only $25,000 there. The bastard had double-crossed him.

The young jury forewoman gathered her nerve.

"The jury finds the defendant not guilty."

The courtroom erupted. Joe Green took advantage of the chaos and bolted out the door, racing to his car. The judge pounded uselessly with his gavel, shouting "Order. Order."

No one listened. Eileen O'Connor felt sick, not triumphant, as she watched Paula Vasquez regain her composure and gallantly walk over to congratulate her.

"I'm so sorry," whispered O'Connor to her opponent.

"I know," said Vasquez. "I know."

Sammie couldn't make her fingers work her phone. Jake Gordon probably knew anyway. The TV networks had broken into regular programming. The Associated Press had sent out bulletin after bulletin. The feminist in Sammie's soul was still somewhat relieved. Of course, an embryo was not a person. But all her work, all that reporting. Kramer was pure evil. And now he was a free man. How could this have happened?

Josie and Peter, surrounded by the protective circle of the IVF mothers, were sleepwalked out of the courtroom, disbelief raging in their minds and hearts. Josie was sobbing. Peter was clutching his stomach with one hand, his other arm shielding his wife.

"He's free. That asshole, that murderer, is free. And Jamie is dead. Our Jamie is dead. Still dead. Forever dead," Peter said louder and louder with each step, to no one in particular.

Outside the courtroom, the demonstrators were out of control. The pro-lifers, some brandishing guns, were an attack mob, rushing the abortion rights supporters, screaming, vowing revenge. Hysterical shouts of "An embryo *is* a person" echoed in the charged air. Police tried desperately to control the melee.

Paula Vasquez, struggling to act more composed than she felt, walked to one of the two microphones set up for the impromptu press conferences on the courthouse steps.

"May I have your attention, please," she spoke clearly, solemnly, into the microphone. It took minutes for the crowd to quiet enough to hear her.

"Today, justice was not served. Dr. Saul Kramer is a murderer and now a free man. The babies he killed have not been avenged. Their deaths have been rendered meaningless. There can never be peace for their parents." As she spoke, Josie and Peter moved to stand beside her on either side, putting their arms around her.

At the other microphone, Eileen O'Connor stood silent, waiting her turn. It came.

"I am so sorry to have won this case," she spoke so softly that the crowd could barely hear her, despite the microphone.

"This is a victory in the sense that the jury has wisely decided that an embryo is not a person. My client, Dr. Saul Kramer, has been exonerated legally. But he is not exonerated morally. Now, against my advice, Dr. Kramer would like to speak to you."

"Murderer! Murderer!" some demonstrators shouted, regardless of their positions on abortion rights.

Kramer, his belly bloated, his steps wobbly, and his face yellow from jaundice, approached the microphone. His mother worked her way to his side, but didn't touch him.

In the back of the crowd, Joe Green, hidden in the masses, slowly raised the gun he had retrieved from the glove compartment in his car.

The sun glinted off its metallic shaft, catching Kramer's mother's eye. As her son started to speak, she saw Green in the crowd and saw his finger tighten on the trigger. Instinctively, she flung herself in front of her son. The bullet pierced her chest, triggering an explosion of bright red blood all over her, her son, and the courthouse steps.

A horrible scream filled the air, drowning out the demonstrators.

"No, Ma, no! No! Ma!" Dr. Saul Kramer, son, Harvard doctor, devil, crumpled over his mother.

His mother looked up at him, her eyes beginning to roll back in her head.

"Ma, I'm dying anyway. I gave myself an injection with the gene. Niemann-Pick."

"Nooooooo," she wailed, trying to focus on her son's face.

The crowd went wild. Brave bystanders tried to wrestle Green to the ground. Sammie stood on stage staring at Kramer's dying mother and at Kramer, whose shoulders shook with grief.

Suddenly, the hairs on Bob Brightman's neck sprang up. He was standing at the back of the crowd, holding Liam's and

Beau's hands. Green had broken free from the men trying to restrain him. Bob spun around and saw Green slowly raising his gun again, this time, aiming directly at Sammie up on stage.

"No," Bob shrieked, dropping the boys' hands and parting the crowd with his arms as if in a desperate breaststroke. He hurled himself at Green, a wild, off-balance tackle. Green lost his balance and his grip on the gun, gasping for breath. Bob's fingers dug deep into Green's pant legs, as they both crashed to the ground.

Grunting, swearing, Bob pinned him down with his own body weight. A crowd encircled the two men. A heavyset gray-haired woman with her purse tucked tightly under one arm squatted to pick up the loose gun with her other hand, her fingers closing on the metal. Her face contorted in disgust as if she held a dirty diaper.

Five policemen pushed frantically through the crowd, guns drawn.

"Get back! Get back!" they yelled as the crowd shrank back. The police pulled Bob off Joe Green and jerked Green's arms, hard, behind his back and handcuffed him. They pulled him to his feet and stiff-walked him to a police car.

Up at the front, surprising herself, Josie gently detached herself from Peter's arm and knelt down beside Kramer's dying mother. Mesmerized now, the crowd hushed. The older woman's body was limp, but her eyelids fluttered as Josie leaned down to whisper in her ear.

"I was a mother, too, once," Josie murmured. "I loved my son, too."

Kramer's mother's eyes opened ever so slightly, trying to find Josie's face.

"Forgive yourself," Josie whispered, a little louder to be sure the old woman heard. "Be at peace."

Peter, who had come close and knelt beside Josie, heard the words. He wondered whether Josie's kind words of peace were meant for Kramer's mother or for herself.

Sammie watched the dying woman's eyes close. Sammie heard her whisper one last word.

"*Danke.*"

BOB AND SAMMIE lay back on the pillows in the king-sized bed, Sammie with her arm around Beau, Bob with his arm around Liam. Bob picked up the remote and flicked off the TV.

"I don't understand," Beau said, snuggling closer to his mom.

"Me neither," echoed Liam.

"It really is hard to understand," Sammie agreed. "I'm still working things out in my head, too."

"Basically, the bad guy got away?" ventured Liam.

"He did, legally," said Bob. "And the reason was a good one. But in a moral sense, I mean, in the sense of right and wrong, everybody knows he was wrong."

"Then why did his mother try to save him when that guy with the gun tried to shoot him?" asked Beau.

"Because she loved him," Sammie answered. "She knew he had done very bad things. She was the one who called the police on him. But he was still her son. And she still loved him."

"Would you love me if I killed someone?" asked Liam.

Sammie had to laugh. "I would, Liam. But, like Dr. Kramer's mother, I'd also call the cops on you. And I would not forgive you. It's complicated."

"What's not complicated," interjected Bob, "is that we are a family and love each other, and that will never change."

The boys snuggled close. Sammie closed her eyes.

EPILOGUE

SEPTEMBER 2020

It was warm, the soft kiss of summer still palpable. The small crowd—masked because of the COVID pandemic—gazed at the handmade altar in the shady backyard of an old friend of Sammie's. Enormous flower vases had been placed on either side of the altar. Sammie stood in front of the altar as calmly as she could, her arms outstretched in welcome. The guests giddily took their seats in the chairs that had been set up in a semicircle six feet apart.

Sammie had been designated minister for the day, certified by the state of Massachusetts to perform the marriage ceremony. She looked out at the guests, many of whom hadn't seen each other since the memorial services for Katy and Jamie.

The mothers from the IVF group were all here, beaming and holding their children on their laps. The lawyers from the

CRISPR trial, Eileen O'Connor and Paula Vasquez, were here, too, sitting side by side, close friends now and partners in the law firm they founded together.

Like all grooms, the tall, fortyish man looked nervous, but handsome. He stood near Sammie facing the crowd, flanked by the only man he knew in this country, now his best man, Peter Northrup.

Chege Mutoka scanned the back of the church, waiting for his bride. As the chamber music quartet flipped pages on their scores to find Mendelssohn's Wedding March, all eyes followed Chege's to the back of the church.

Down the aisle, slightly unsure, but smiling gamely as instructed, two young girls from Kenya, ages eight and ten, distributed rose petals as they walked slowly to the front. Chege's nieces had been orphaned when both their parents died of AIDS. Dressed in identical yellow dresses with garlands of flowers tipping perilously off their heads, the girls, Elizabeth and Diana, were now the newly adopted daughters of Ashlyn Wilson and Chege Mutoka.

Ashlyn had met and fallen in love with Chege, a physician specializing in malaria, last year in Kenya. After finishing up their project, Ashlyn and Chege had brought the girls home to Ashlyn's too-small condo in Somerville.

A few steps behind the flower girls, also in yellow, came the radiantly pregnant matron of honor, Josie Northrup.

Her cocktail-length dress swished flirtatiously around her calves as she walked down the aisle. She and Peter had finally used the other IVF clinic and, in the first cycle, had gotten pregnant. Their baby, a little girl, was due in three months. Up front next to Chege, Peter returned Josie's grin, every bit as deliriously happy as his wife.

As she passed them, grinning in un-matronly glee, Josie winked at her IVF group friends in the congregation.

Finally, as the music swelled, came Ashlyn, escorted gallantly, if a bit awkwardly, by Sammie's boys, Liam and Beau, one on each side. The formality of their brand-new tuxedoes clashed charmingly with the everyday-ness of their just-scrubbed, sunburned faces.

In a deep-cut, cream silk gown with a long train that floated gracefully behind her, Ashlyn smiled at her soon-to-be husband. She was radiant.

Sammie opened her notes to begin the ceremony. Nothing that had happened in the last year, not even the pandemic, had made her religious, but at this moment, she felt something close: overwhelming gratitude.

Just yesterday, Jake Gordon, who sat prominently in the front row, had told her that her stories on Saul Kramer would be submitted for this year's Pulitzer Prize for public service, the most prestigious of the Pulitzer categories. And just last week had come the news that Kramer had been found dead, alone, in his mother's apartment, where he had spent the last months of his life. His children had never talked to him, though they had arranged to have his condo fees paid and for a shopping service to deliver groceries once a week. They also paid, with the money from selling his house, for a visiting nurse to come every other day, though it had proved difficult to find and keep nurses willing to tend to a dying murderer.

Sammie had dutifully noted the grisly details of Kramer's death in a front-page story in the *Times*, including the fact that the medical examiner had found a cherry-red spot on Kramer's retinas, the hallmark of Niemann-Pick. Sammie felt no joy in realizing that Kramer had injected himself with the deadly gene, probably on the very day her first story had run.

Sammie had covered Joe Green's murder trial as well, feeling grimly satisfied when the jury found him guilty of the murder of Jan Schwartz Kramer.

As Ashlyn and Chege clasped hands and looked expectantly at her, Sammie glanced at the back of the church where Ricardo and Heather sat, accompanied by Ricardo's wife and their child. Ricardo and Heather were now co-chiefs of Kramer's old lab, eagerly pursuing research on Niemann-Pick.

Next week, they would start the first human trials using CRISPR to do what it had always been intended to do and the opposite of what Kramer had done—they would take out the deadly Niemann-Pick gene in potential embryos that had been tested and shown to carry it and insert a healthy gene instead.

Grinning from ear to ear, Sammie watched as Ashlyn and Chege exchanged vows and rings. The congregation held its collective breath as the couple indulged in a long, happy embrace.

At Sammie's discreet signal, the organist crouched in the bell tower made the bells ring out.

The congregation erupted, swarming the newly married pair as they walked slowly out of the church into the sunshine.

AUTHOR'S NOTE

For the record, as a science and medical journalist and author, I am strongly in favor of CRISPR and other developments in medical research. But we also need public discussion of the potential ethical pitfalls of this remarkable new technology. Hence this book.

ABOUT THE AUTHOR

Judy Foreman is a former *Boston Globe* health columnist and the author of three works of nonfiction. A Wellesley College grad (Phi Beta Kappa), she spent three years as a Peace Corps Volunteer in Brazil and holds a Master's from the Harvard Graduate School of Education. She was a Lecturer on Medicine at Harvard Medical School, a Fellow in Medical Ethics, also at Harvard Medical School, a Knight Science Fellow at MIT, and a Senior Fellow at the Schuster Institute for Investigative Journalism at Brandeis University. She has won more than fifty journalism awards including a George Foster Peabody Award and a Science in Society Award from the National Association of Science Writers. She lives outside of Boston. *CRISPR'd* is her first novel.